"Yes, he is rich. Therefore, *we* are also rich."

"Egon, your eggs are several years old, and we are so not rich."

He looks at his plate. His eggs are not scrambled, they are fried. But it's still early and I am afraid I have confused him.

It's a rare morning when Egon, Meredith, and I are sitting together having breakfast. She's made us bacon and eggs and toast and fried tomatoes.

"I'm not eating those," Egon says, pointing at the tomatoes as if they have just slithered under the door out of the backyard.

"So don't," Meredith says. "Who cares about your nutrition and whether your brain ever attains its full size."

"I have attained my full brain size already," Egon says.

She reaches across the table and pats his hand. "Oh, you poor thing."

"Meredith, will you explain to the poor thing that we are not anywhere near rich, and we never will be?"

"We are not rich, Thing, and we never will be."

"Speak for yourselves. I'm going to be rich, that's for sure."

Praise for THE BIG GAME OF EVERYTHING

"I have read every book Chris Lynch has published. I love his work. He is a guy's guy and a writer's writer. With THE BIG GAME OF EVERYTHING I read it three times. It's that good. As he says in the novel, 'you can't choose your family.' However, you can choose what to read—and THE BIG GAME OF EVERYTHING is the novel version of a blood brother."
—Jack Gantos, author of JOEY PIGZA SWALLOWED THE KEY and HOLE IN MY LIFE

"Funny and touching, with a rapport between two brothers that zings like lightning."
—Ned Vizzini, author of IT'S KIND OF A FUNNY STORY, BE MORE CHILL, and TEEN ANGST? NAAAH . . .

"THE BIG GAME OF EVERYTHING is a funny, thoughtful novel that considers the true nature of class, happiness, and success through the eyes of a teenage boy."
—SLJ

"Lynch is adept at creating physical comedy on the printed page, conjuring vivid scenes of mad, elderly golf-cart drivers and a (literal) wild goose chase around a water hazard. The motley group of eccentric characters, set loose on a giant playground complete with grown-up-sized toys, makes for a welcome getaway."

—*The Horn Book*

"A subtle portrait of family tendencies and their consequences, neatly tucked into a rich and immediately satisfying story of brotherly mayhem; readers may even be moved to look beyond their own surface readings of their families as a result."

—*BCCB*

"This Printz Honor–winning author offers up another touching and offbeat novel full of delightfully skewed humor. Readers will likely consider their place—and evaluate their need to participate—in 'the big game of everything' in their own lives."

—*VOYA*

"This offbeat story will appeal to anyone with a funny bone."

—*KLIATT*

Also by Chris Lynch

Shadow Boxer
Iceman
Gypsy Davey
Political Timber
Slot Machine
Extreme Elvin
Whitechurch

The Blue-Eyed Son Trilogy:
Mick
Blood Relations
Dog Eat Dog

Gold Dust
Freewill
All the Old Haunts
Who the Man
The Gravedigger's Cottage
Me, Dead Dad, & Alcatraz
Sins of the Fathers

THE BIG GAME OF EVERYTHING

CHRIS LYNCH

HARPER TEEN

An Imprint of HarperCollinsPublishers

HarperTeen is an imprint of HarperCollins Publishers.

The Big Game of Everything

Library of Congress Cataloging-in-Publication Data
Lynch, Chris.
The Big Game of Everything / Chris Lynch. — 1st ed.
    p. cm.
Summary: Jock and his eccentric family spend the summer working
at Grampus's golf complex, where they end up learning the rules of
"The Big Game of Everything."
  ISBN 978-0-06-074036-8
[1. Family life—Fiction. 2. Grandfathers—Fiction. 3. Summer
employment—Fiction. 4. Golf—Fiction.] I. Title.
PZ7.L979739Bi 2008   2007049578
[Fic]—dc22   CIP
                                                  AC

Typography by Jennifer Heuer
10   11   12   13   14   LP/CW   10 9 8 7 6 5 4 3 2 1
❖

First paperback edition, 2010

THE BIG GAME OF EVERYTHING

1

D'YA LOVE ME?

You have to love your family. You do, even if you don't, right? You don't have to agree with them or appreciate them or go to concerts with them or even understand them, but you have to love them. It's a rule, and it's the kind of rule you don't break unless you're some kind of animal.

I do love my brother, but I don't know that I would if I were not required to. We're not the same. It can happen in a family. Even though you get all the same genetic stuff, and you get raised in the same setup, you can wind up seeing and feeling things a whole different way from the guy just one bed over. It's kind of crazy, when you think about it, but it's nature's way. The payback, I guess, is that while you have to love your family, your family has to love you too, no matter what.

"Ya? Who says?"

2

UNION

Union Jack. You think it's from a flag, probably, or a song or something. Well, it isn't, it's from where most loony things come from: inside my parents' heads. Only I have bent it so that it is pronounced with a short *u* sound, and an *o* where the *a*'s supposed to be so you say it like this, Onion Jock, even though you write it, if you decide you want to write to me, like this, Union Jack. No country would call its flag Onion Jock.

My parents are likewise confused, thinking my name comes from a flag. They say they gave me that name after I was conceived during a dreamy stay in the city of York, England, but does anybody anywhere want to hear the word *conceived* coming from their parents? That's right, they don't. So when they told me this when I was about six, dragging me against my will into their hippy-frippy universe where everything is cool and sayable, I turned right around and dragged them back down into mine, where a certain amount is cool but I'll be the judge of that.

"Onion," I said.

"Onion?" Mom said. They looked at each other and back to me again.

"Onion," I said. "It's pronounced *Onion Jock*."

Got them right back on their heels there. They just kept blinking at me like I had turned a big turbine fan in their faces, and I kept blinking right back, so it's not like we were testing to see who would blink first.

Then, they smiled. At me. At each other. At the cosmic crazy wonder of life or something like that. They didn't say exactly, but I've learned how to read this kind of doolally on their faces, so I know that's what they were thinking.

You'd expect to blow your folks away, changing your name only six years after they gave it to you. That would be if your folks were regular. My folks are irregular. You can't blow them away because they are like wispy multicolored autumn leaves that you can blow at all you want but they still come swirling back to settle down in the corner of your yard up against the fence.

They're freaks, my folks, that's why they talk like that, that's why they named me like that, that's why they act like they do. They have impulse control problems that follow us around forever after. They are dear, sweet freaks beloved by all, but that does not make them any less freakish.

And it's my name, so I can do what I like with it. But I was surprised to find that once I changed it, everyone went along.

"That's a fat lie. It's pronounced *Onion* because of the smell."

That's not me telling you that. That's my spokes-devil, who is always with me even when he's not. He's my brother, whose name is Egon, which doesn't involve flags at all unless perhaps hell has a flag. There is some disagreement about the origin of his name, with my mother saying it came from a restaurant guide that steered them to some very lovely meals when they traveled across Europe after college, and my father saying it came from the film *Ghostbusters*. Egon hates everybody because he thinks everybody is a dingleberry, and while he may be right a lot of the time, I don't let it bother me as much as he lets it bother him.

"That's because you're a dingleberry," Egon says.

He's not as bad as he sounds. I tell myself that a lot. It's something like a mantra that my parents—who are highly mantra-type people—taught me very early on when it started becoming apparent that he was exactly as bad as he sounded. He's not as bad as he sounds, though.

"Yes, I am. D'ya love me?"

That's the mantra they gave Egon. Hardly seems like a fair exchange, does it? And being him, he has managed to turn it into a blunt instrument to beat me with. "D'ya love me?" he asks through his demented grin.

"Of course," I say. "It's the law."

Egon is a year younger than me and about thirty pounds heavier than me and ever since we were in the first years of school everybody new figured he was the big brother. He got his build from my mother's side of the family—stocky, solid, substantial—while I got mine from my dad's—wiry. One time, when we were all at a cheesy carnival together, some kid we didn't even know made a remark that my parents looked like a number ten together, and Egon beat the kid nearly unconscious with a plastic SpongeBob SquarePants. The same could be said for how Egon and I look, though you'd have trouble finding anyone to say it.

"I am the big brother," he says.

Well, yes, he is. But more importantly, I am the older brother.

"Who says that's more important?"

It's just one of those things everybody understands.

"I don't understand it."

There, but for that thirty pound weight difference, would be where I would say it doesn't take a big fancy idea for you not to understand it, Egon.

I have now summoned his devil voice. "What did you say?" You know the voice, sounds like the devil? It complements his flushed devil face, sharp-angled eyebrows, pale eyes, tight whitish hair. His features look like he's always leaning into a mighty headwind.

Nothing, Egon. Maybe you're right. Maybe being older isn't the most important.

"Are you calling me stupid?"

Of course I'm not. I'm saying you're right. Being older is not more important. We are equal partners.

"Yes it is, and no we're not. I'm older now so forget the equality."

Excuse me?

"I'm the older one now. It's my turn. You've been at it long enough, and you're crap. No more bossing me around."

It has been years since I even attempted to do anything you could really call bossing. So I don't suppose the age-exchange will make any noticeable difference to my life.

But I don't have to take it lying down exactly.

If you get to be the older one, does that mean I get to be the stupid one now, Egon?

. . . .
. . . .
. . . .
. . . .

That's us fighting now. It gets physical sometimes. Just a second . . . .
. . . .
. . . .
. . . .
. . . .
. . . .

You would think after learning all you have learned about us so far, that Union Jack would be powder after one round with Egon Devil. You would, however, be failing to recognize the historic brotherly banjax that makes a fight between siblings so much more fun and interesting than it would otherwise be. Take this example: Brother Egon fights casual rival we will refer to as Dingleberry A. Brother Egon makes a sidewalk splotch out of him. Soon thereafter, hapless unlucky Brother Jock runs into same Dingleberry A. Dingleberry A, in physical and emotional pain, lays a beating on entirely innocent Brother Jock who, in fairness, was weakened by a bad cold that day, but still.

"You tell the most boring stories. Even a story with all the good stuff this story has, you go and make a snore out of it. Tell it better or I'm going to tell it myself."

Right. So, reasonably outraged at the unfairness of life, Brother Jock stomps home and, finding the brother who is responsible, promptly and violently feeds him his lunch.

"Oh, please, I was actually eating my lunch at the time."

Still. Still, it was a thrashing.

"It was no thrashing."

It was a scuffing, then.

"Okay. I can live with that, you did give me a scuffing."

So how can this be? How does he beat up a guy who beats up me, then I go and beat up him? That monkeys with the rules of the universe, doesn't it? How?

"Because he's my bro. He's my bronion."

Yes, that's it. We are bronions.

"We stench."

We don't stench.

But you know what my bronion did after I came home and gave him a thrashing?

"A scuffing."

A scuffing. Know what he did?

"I went out and tracked down Dingleberry A again, didn't I? Nobody touches my bronion but me."

That's what it is, you know. It's love.

"No it isn't."

What is it then?

"I don't know, but it's something else. So don't say that again."

Broniony love.

Excuse us . . . .
. . . .
. . . .
. . . .

We collect golf balls at the driving range for a living. We're not officially supposed to have a living yet because we're not old enough, but we do anyway. My grampus owns the driving range and thirteen-hole course alongside it (he's been adding a hole at a time at a leisurely pace), so he can employ us as he sees fit and for whatever wages he deems fit. He doesn't even deem it fit to be consistent. Some weeks he pays us a dollar an hour, some weeks ten. And the truth is, we do more than just collect balls. We do everything.

We've done this off and on for a few years, but now it steps up a level. For while some kids go away to the country, to farms or seasides for their vacations, my brother and I get to spend the summer full-time, all season, roaming the wilds of our grandfather's golf course kingdom.

We've been waiting for this forever.

"I'm not even going to go back to school in the fall, if this works out."

You are of course going back to school. He is going back to school, no matter how great this works out. Egon has a plan already, to finish school and go to the police academy. He wants to be a cop when he's older because he says he likes to beat people up and tell them what's wrong with them.

"You're a dingleberry," he says, and punches me in the kidney.

There are a lot, a lot of great things about running the golf complex—Grampus loves to call it that, the *complex*, even though it's a pretty simple place. It's got the course and the range, an indoor/outdoor café, a function room next to the café that has a few video games and a mighty fine pool table that he demands we call a snooker table and a TV that hangs from the ceiling, a pro shop for all the rank amateurs who play here, and lots of free-range roaming kid space in the woods that ride the hills that ring the *complex*.

If you were twelve or thirteen and were going to build a place to get your jollies for the summer and make one to ten dollars an hour doing it, this would be that place.

Which brings us to probably the coolest part of working the complex for the summer. The great big twelve-year-old who actually *did* build it: my grandfather. Aka Grampus, aka Grumpus.

"Aka Old Man Dingleberry."

Nobody calls him that except Egon, except even Egon doesn't call him that.

"It's true, I don't."

Grampus is as undingleberrylike as you can get if you are that age. He has the greatest life, running the complex, tooling around in one of the two golf carts we have, or digging stuff up with his mini backhoe. He doesn't even love golf that much and only got his own course after getting some decent dough off his invention. It's a little trailer attachment for the back of a golf cart that scoops up golf balls but also happened to work like a demon for picking up rubbish and dog business from parks and parking lots. In his semi-retirement Grampus made a healthy buck or two cleaning up big yards and small parks for as far as he could get on his little golf cart before he went and sold his patent and bought his complex, and now he spends his spare time working on all his other invention ideas that are never going to help anyone anywhere do anything.

It's been like a second life for him, after working his whole adult life for the marines and then the city parks department. He's boss now, and he owns stuff, and he likes that because it is so different from everything that came before.

"I already thought he was cool before because he was the only person I knew with his own golf cart."

Indeed. That would always have been enough for

us. But now, we have golf cart *world*. It really is a golf cart world for us now, thanks to the old man.

Grampus even takes old ladies on golf cart dates around the complex in his nice suit on warm summer nights, catching up on showing off. He has been divorced from our grammus for long enough that the situation doesn't seem to bother anybody involved, which is nice. We suspect he will not remarry, no matter how nice some of the golf cart ladies are.

"I've had more marriages already than I care to recall," he said the one time I asked about his intentions.

This came as a surprise. "How many?" I asked.

"One," he said.

There was a golf cart lady sitting in the cart when he said it. We didn't see her again after that. It's possible I shouldn't have brought it up just then.

It was agreed that Egon and I would do every kind of odd job necessary around the complex for the entire summer.

"The odder the better" was Egon's way of seeing things.

What we didn't know was that we would be running just about everything. I wasn't all that sure we would be up to the job of everything.

"What are you whimpering about?" Grampus said. "By the time I was your age I was playing semi-pro football, I had my own beach house which I built myself, and I rode a Harley Davidson to school. Two strapping sprogs like you around, why should I have to hire all kinds of summer help to get things done?"

Grampus is not a free-spending kind of a guy.

"Jock was whimpering, Grampus," Egon said, "not me."

That's the kind of solidarity that will see us through.

3

BUCKET O' BALLS

We even handle our own transportation. The road, two lanes and three miles of rolling, bending hill between our house and the complex, is not suited to cycling. But we are, so it's okay. Treacherous, but okay.

It doesn't have to be as hairy a trip as it is. Egon makes it more adventurous by insisting on wearing both headphones and the spiked golf shoes he got out of the complex's lost and found, which he treats as his own personal footlocker.

"Turn it off," I shout as we crest the highest of the hills and start into our downswoop. I have pulled up beside him on the road side, the dangerous side, to try and get his attention. I do not get his attention. He plays his music so loud you can hear it from six feet away. He plays it so loud the drivers speeding past us can surely hear it, and it's probably drowning out their own radios, which is possibly why they are driving like they want to make roadkill out of us. And his music is awful even when you turn it down. I've tried it at home, and I swear it turns itself back up.

To make matters worse, Egon's attention is caught by a butterfly or a shapely rock or something dead that causes him to look in the direction of the grassy off-road.

I should just let him get run over, shouldn't I? Sometimes I think I do way too much work keeping my brother on the upright side of downwrong and I should just leave him at the mercy of himself.

But you know and I know I'm not going to do that. You and I and he all know that.

So I drift back, pull behind and around him, and come up close on the inside.

He snaps his puggy face up at me like I just dropped from a spaceship and was not here all along. He has been bobbing his head to some monstrosity of a tuneless tune and now he is not bobbing and not pleased about it because I have spoiled his world. He's glaring at me, not even looking at the road as we shoot down it at about thirty miles an hour.

I am watching the road. And him. And the road. The road is going awfully fast. And the cars, of course, the cars are going even faster.

"I am *ordering* you to turn that thing off," I shout. "You can't even tell when the cars are coming. You almost got run over three times already."

I did say he was cycling in golf spikes, right? Which make things even more dangerous.

With one smooth up-and-out stroke, like a circus bike acrobat, my brother lifts his inside, me-side, foot off the pedal, extends, and kicks. With the spikes, into my knee, which hits the bike frame, which wobbles the front wheel, which throws the balance just enough . . .

I am off the road and onto the grass, and I am bouncing. I'm bouncing like one of those ski jumpers who wipe out in a terrible crash and they slow it down for you on TV so everybody can appreciate how gimpy and lifeless and hilarious his limbs and head are as they bounce, bounce, bounce along the surface of whatever surface will have them. Only the ski jumpers have snow to slide over, and I have patchy tough public works grass and rocks and rubbish, and a bike that punches itself right into my back at the end.

Oh, and the sound of a brother cackling like a flock

of seagulls over a French fry as he turns the corner toward the complex, undoubtedly to fink to Grampus that I am late and he is not. Ski jumpers don't have that.

It takes a while to walk the half-mile approach road that leads to the complex, because my bike and I want to give each other a break. We tromp past the sheep and chickens making soft sympathetic noises at us from the other side of the fence along the way. It is breezy but warm, partly sunny, mostly quiet, and it smells like soft midsummer. It's a beautiful lonesome road, this road, and I like that I can look directly up at the sky and walk straight ahead and feel safe and fine doing it as long as my brother's not nearby. I've almost forgotten the accident as I park my bike, and I suck it all in before walking into the pro shop to start my working vacation.

"Sergeant Dingleberry, you're late," Grampus says from behind the counter. "Should've come along with your brother, who's hard at work already. Shouldn't have stayed in bed, should ya?"

Oh ya, he finked.

"Sorry, Grampus."

"So you work the first hour for free. And clean the toilets."

"What's Egon doing?"

He smiles like he has a secret and waves me over close to him. "Egon's giving the junior golf lesson," he says.

"Giving a lesson? Egon doesn't even know how to golf."

"Ya, but he's got the shoes. They give him authority."

"They do not."

"No, they don't. But truth is, it's not even really a lesson. It's more like day care. It's all the little ones brought along by the ladies group, to whom *I* give the real lesson." The real lesson is more like a tea party for all involved, where Grampus gets to peacock for the ladies and they get to stroll around and goof off in the sun while my brother mentally damages their children for an hour.

I love my grandfather's life. I want it.

"Does Egon know all this?"

"He knows as much as he needs to know," Grampus says, giving me a wink. Right now he's out on the range with a bucket o' balls, trying to learn how to hit a ball before his pupils show up. "Go clean those bathrooms. Then, after the kids come and golf and eat and horrify the bathroom all over again, it'll be your brother's turn to clean it."

Now *that's* an even better day.

"Why am I getting all the breaks, Grampus?"

"Because your hand is bleeding, and you have a grass stain on your forehead, and I don't like finkage."

He is a great man.

I can smile as I head to the toilets. "So you really are going to pay me for the hour, then."

"Nope," he says brightly.

He is a pretty good man.

I shouldn't say Egon and I run everything. There's Grampus, of course, and he helps. And there's Meredith, our sister, who has everything. She's very smart, not like a genius, but like a clever, wily kind of smart that means she gets whatever she wants. She is, I suppose, some version of pretty that I cannot exactly see, based on the attention of hundreds of boyfriends over the years and that mystery power certain types of females have over gas station attendants and traffic cops and Christmas tree salesmen who fall over themselves to do exactly what she wants them to do just because she's there. She is tall and zit-free and plays tennis like a machine. She has long wavy hair in a shade somewhere between copper and bronze that I have not seen anywhere else, and it manages always to look like it is flowing, the way a person's hair looks when they are underwater. There are a lot of reasons to hate Meredith. She has just graduated high school, so she's a big shot and a big pain and her graduation ceremony was the most boring seventy-five hours of my life topped by the fact that she received a *scooter* for her graduation from my parents.

She didn't graduate from my parents. She graduated from school. She received a scooter from my parents. Because she graduated from school. She wouldn't want to graduate from my parents, because they get along great. That's why she received such a gem of a graduation present from them. Because when I say scooter I don't mean the kind of thing you push along with one foot and that has wheels the size of doughnuts, I mean this beautiful gold Honda 50cc pleasure machine that has storage and a windshield and is highway-able and elevates its owner above ever having to take a bicycle onto dangerous roads again.

"I told you he tells the most boring stories, didn't I? Dingleberry, why do you have to clog up every story with fifty million details on top of the information that matters?"

My brother has kindly decided to visit me on the

floor of the bathroom, which is now the cleanest place in the complex.

"Shouldn't you be teaching golf to a bunch of six-year-olds?"

"Yes, I should. But I lost a couple of them and I need help finding them."

"You lost a couple."

"That's what I said."

"How many did you start with?"

"Three."

"I'd think you'd be a little more concerned."

"You would, wouldn't ya?"

"So if you're not bothered, why are you here bothering me?"

"Because if I don't find them, Grampus is going to take them out of my pay."

True enough. Heartless all around, but true.

"What do I care about your pay? Because of you, he docked an hour off mine."

"Okay, help me find the two slugbundles I lost and I'll give you a buck."

I put out my hand. I'm no chump.

"I don't have any dough on me," he says.

"Then find your own slugbundles. What did you do with the third one, anyway?"

"I left him chasing ducks around the first hole water hazard with a one-iron."

"Oh, that's good. You've got it all under control, then."

I go back to making the porcelain glow. Off in the distance there is a scream.

"Fine," Egon says, pulling out a crumply buck and throwing it at me.

"Sorry," I say, "that scream makes this a level-two situation, which costs two bucks."

He reaches in and pulls out another crumpled bill and pelts me with it. I compare it with the first. They are crumpled perfectly the same, tight like golf balls. He keeps them that way for moments like these for, like his grandfather, he does not separate painlessly from his money.

"Do you work on these?" I ask. "It's like a kind of angry origami."

"It'll be angry origami when I bend you into seven different animal shapes."

There's another scream. Egon shoves a third dollar into my hand, lifts me right up off the floor, and drags me off to the course.

We follow the scream down to the water hazard at one. There, we find what must be one of the golf mothers running after a mad posse of geese, who are likewise chasing after a little kid with a one-iron. Everybody involved in this chase scene is furious and spewing feathers as they circle the little pond. Honks and squawks and cries of "Mommy" fill the air, and I would surely be falling down laughing if we were not up to our necks in involvement.

Egon has fallen off the pace and is now behind me. Falling down laughing.

I turn back to find him on his knees.

"This might be the funniest thing I have ever seen," he says.

"This is *your* responsibility," I shout at him.

"Hey," Egon shouts back, "it's his own fault. I told him he could chase the ducks but not the geese. I specifically told him not the geese."

"Great. What is he, *six*?"

"How would I know? He's a *kid*. They all look the same."

"Go save him, Egon. I'll look for the other two."

"Where you gonna look?"

A voice the size of Montana starts bellowing down at the driving range.

"Hey you, get out of there! What are you doing out there? Can't you read the signs? You're not supposed

to be out there! You wanna get killed? Where are your parents?"

"I guess I'll try the driving range," I say.

Egon runs down to do battle with the geese and probably with that kid's mother while I run to the range.

"Get out of there, kid, I mean it."

The guy is still yelling, but I can't see any kid he could be yelling at. The range is like a big cage three football fields long. I run along the high mesh fence beside the range, down to the bank of bays where the golfers hit from. He's the only person here yet, in bay nine out of the fifteen. I run right up to his bay, which normally you should never do to a golfer, especially a screamer.

"What's the problem, sir?"

"The problem," he says, pointing his jumbo Big Bertha driver out into the distance, "is that little prairie dog you got right out there in the middle of your driving range."

I follow his line and locate the prairie dog.

He's not, really. He's a kid. But he looks enough like one, small, narrow, dark-eyed. And he's doing that cute standing thing they do with their heads perked way up and their little hand things hanging in front of them. He's sort of in a prairie dog den, too, one of three semicircular target pits Grampus recently dug and shaped and lined with bright yellow plastic for the golfers to practice accurate mid-range approach shots.

"Well, he's not supposed to be in there," I say.

"Well, I know that," he says, "*I* can read."

There is a sign at each and every one of the fifteen driving bays that says "Please do not step out onto the driving range for any reason at any time."

"He's kind of small," I say. "Probably not that great at reading yet."

"Probably that one's not, either," he says, pointing thirty yards to the right, to another yellow target and another prairie dog.

"Sorry, sir, my brother was supposed to be watching them but he let them slip away."

"What are you people running here now, a day care?"

"My grandfather says it doesn't count as day care if they're getting a golf lesson, so we're okay."

Now the guy just stares at me.

"I'll go get them out of your way," I say.

And against orders, against obvious and visible

signage telling me not to, I run straight out onto that driving range.

Prairie dogs can be surprisingly hard to catch. It takes me what seems like an hour to round up the two little critters because they do not seem to want to be rounded up, no matter what. Twice I catch one dog and have to haul him around on my shoulder while I chase the other one. It hurts my back. They run around flags, back toward the bays, back out all the way to the 250-yard marker, all the time screaming, "No, no! I *hate* golf. Golf is so boring. You can't make me."

I feel bad. I don't have any argument for them because golf *is* boring if you're six. But if they don't get taken care of, then their mothers don't come for lessons, then Grampus doesn't get to flirt with them and get paid for it, then I don't get paid by him, then I have to spend the summer sweeping up hair in my dad's barbershop. You want to talk about boring? If I could force these two to work in the barbershop they'd soon run out screaming and begging for their putters.

"Get over here, prairie dog," I shout, and finally grab the second one by a hind leg and bring him down like today's coyote lunch.

"I'm sorry, guys," I say, carrying one on each shoulder back toward the clubhouse. "I'm just doing my job."

They kick, they squirm, they squeal.

"Dingleberry," one of them shouts.

"Ya," his partner adds. "Dingleberry. You're a dingleberry."

"Ya, mister dingleberry."

"Well," I say, "I see he's taught you *something*."

I and mine hook up with Egon and his back at the café. I instantly burst out laughing as I see the big angry welt on his forehead. My captives squiggle down me like they're climbing down a tree, and run to the corner of the café where the mothers are gathered.

"Mom, I hate this."

"Mom, golf stinks."

"He's a dingleberry."

"Both of them are dingleberries. I hate it here and I never want to come back."

Well, you don't get a report card like that every day.

"These guys are feisty," I say to Egon.

"At least yours were unarmed," he says.

I walk up close to Egon. I examine his head in

detail, the outside, anyway. I can just about make out the little numeral one indented in the groove.

"The little guy has a pretty good stroke already," I say.

"If by 'little guy' you mean Grampus, then yes, he does."

4

PEST CONTROL

One of the more colorful and frightening jobs around
the complex is slathering the factor 2000 sunscreen on
the stringy leathery parts of Grampus that he cannot
reach himself. All it takes is a day above fifty degrees
and the slightest peek of halfhearted sun and he's off
with the shirt for the whole day and on with the sunblock. He's about as okay for it as a 178-year-old guy
can be because he's an ex-military man, outdoorsy,
and always kept himself busy and fit. But still. It's
not a pleasant job, and it goes to the guy who is most
clearly in the doghouse, and if nobody is in the doghouse when the evil sunshine snaps at us then it goes

to me because he says I have the softer hands.

"You know," he says as I grease him up on a lovely hazy seventy-two-degree day, "your hands remind me of your grandmother's. She had superior hands, that woman."

I'm not sure exactly how I want to object to the direction of this conversation, but I know I want to object to it. Having my hands compared to my grandmother's does nothing for me, manliness-wise, and if Egon is in earshot this is going to cost me. And then there's the thought that I'm even doing a job that once was assigned to his wife. And apparently doing it well enough to make him nostalgic for her. Urg.

"Thanks, Grampus."

"Ah, she was great, before she was rotten. Did you know she was a cheerleading coach for the legendary, undefeated 1972 Miami Dolphins and their equally legendary cheerleaders?"

I knew this.

"Ya, Grampus," I say. "How come we don't see her anymore?"

"Ah, she lives in Florida now. Lives with the 1972 Miami Dolphins, in fact."

"All of them?"

"All the ones who are alive and not in jail, sure."

"You are making that up."

"You do have soft hands, though."

When Egon does the sunblock job, he does it badly on purpose so that Grampus will make me do it. He gets sand in the cream and slaps it on in a haphazard way so that some of the sun is blocked but lots of the sun is waved right on through. Last time it was really sunny, Grampus wound up looking like one of those charts in a doctor's office that shows you all the muscles in the human body.

"Buttering up the old man again, I see," says Egon, strolling into the office just as I'm finishing up.

"At least he's doing something," Grampus says. "What have you been up to?"

"Working on my swing," Egon says, miming a smooth stroke. "Gotta keep on top of it if I'm going to be the golf pro at this club."

"You're not the golf pro. You're the babysitter. And now you're not even that because nobody will bring their kids here after you and the geese terrorized them all."

Grampus is now pacing back and forth behind the counter of the pro shop. He looks intimidating, muscular, and shiny now that I've slicked him up like a pro bodybuilder, and it's unnerving the way he's chopping and grabbing at the air.

"You okay, Grampus?" I ask.

"Yes," he says, pacing still. He picks up two handfuls of old practice balls out of a basket on the floor. He squeezes and bobbles them, drops a couple, leaves them as he paces and bobbles some more. "No. I could be better. Business could be better. Not that I *need* the money . . ."

He doesn't. The complex is barely more than a full-time hobby for him. He does not need money as far as I can see.

He admires money. He respects money. He covets, craves, yearns for money.

But he does not need it. My dad always says nobody needs it. My grandfather says my father's insane.

"Money matters, boys. Money matters a great deal, and don't let anyone tell you otherwise. It matters in the way people treat you, it matters in what you get out of life. It matters to how you feel about yourself."

"See, that's what I'm always saying, Grampus," Egon says, "my parents are nuts."

"Yes, they are. And frankly, so far you boys have displayed an unfortunate gift for driving business in the opposite direction, which does not help, money-wise. Look around you here. What do you see?"

"Nothing," Egon says.

"Correct. A lovely morning like this, we should be filling up quick. I mean, we're doing all right, and we will be busy enough later on, but I want us to start making better use of the hours. I want us to be busy in here all the time. I have the staff, after all, so we can cater to thousands."

"Thousands, Grampus?"

"Thousands."

"But there's just the three of us."

"Four. Your sister'll be here today."

"Then you'll really be on your own," I say. "She'll just make us do stuff for *her*."

"No offense, Grampus," Egon says with no apparent ill will, "but I think you're a big suitcase full of senile dementia."

"Hah," the old man answers, tossing all the balls back in the bucket, "and you are a shoebox full of juvenile dementia. Nothing wrong with that. That's the engine that's going to power this great machine of ours.

"Right," Grampus says, clapping his hands together as if we are wrapping up a big business meeting where we just hatched an airtight plan of action.

He even attempts a celebratory hop over the counter.

He does a little run up, plants his hands on the counter to vault over, gets his legs only just to the surface, then plops there with a firm bump. His hip lands hard, then his freshly stripped and greased upper body skitters and scatters all over the place as he fights for balance and control but instead wipes out the stack of gloves and boxes of balls and score cards and brochures, taking the whole carefully arranged setup crashing to the floor with him.

We rush to him.

Well, no, I rush to him. Egon applauds.

"You okay, Grampus?" I ask, trying to get a purchase on his slippery arm.

"Of course I am," he says, standing quickly but listing to one side. It is like limping while standing still. "I was a marine, for heaven's sake."

At this moment, we hear the cool putt-vroom of Meredith's scooter coming to a skidding stop just outside in the gravel parking lot. She crunches across and soon stands in the doorway.

Balls, literature, and gloves are scattered all over. Egon is red with laughter and the marine half naked and glistening in front of me is tilting even farther to one side but trying not to. He puts one hand on a hip and waves feebly to Meredith with the other. He looks just like he's going to sing her "I'm a Little Teacup."

"Did I miss a party?" she asks.

"No," Grampus says, "we were just brainstorming new business ideas."

"These are your business partners now, are they Gramps?"

"Well, not quite, but I'm grooming them. Which brings us to . . ." He takes his teapot spout hand and points it at me. " . . . your grooming. You need to start by getting a haircut, mister Onion Jock."

"Hah," Egon says.

Egon can say hah. Because Egon, just like his grandfather in his marine days, favors a military hairstyle with angles as distinct as the Pentagon's, so nobody's ever going to insist he get his hair cut. Though Grampus, with his horrible geometric atrocity of a varnished comb-over, shouldn't be handing out hair advice.

"And you"—Grampus points at him now—"don't you say hah. You will get yourself a decent shave, mister."

Yes, my younger brother shaves already and I don't. He doesn't shave often enough, even.

"Beoh!" Meredith lets out a cross between a

squeal and a bark as she hops backward right out of the building.

"Gramps," she calls from outside, "I just saw a very large mouse or a not-very-small rat."

Grampus nods. "That's Reggie. He is smarter than me and he is tougher than me and I believe he may be having some impact on our repeat-business problem in the café. That's why these two lads, after they cycle to your father's shop to get themselves cleaned up, are going to continue on to the hardware store to pick up some kind of solution to our Reggie problem."

He pulls out a twenty-dollar bill and waves it in my direction until Egon leaps across and grabs it like an orca doing tricks at SeaWorld.

"What kind of solution?" I ask.

He waves us away with a little two-hand brushing motion in the air. "You're working men with real jobs, fully functioning members of the staff here. You don't need me to lead you by the hand to sort everything out."

"Cool," Egon says. "We'll get a crossbow."

"No weaponry," Grampus says calmly.

"My parents have to say that to him every time he leaves the house," Meredith says.

"Lethal but legal," Grampus says as we slide past

Meredith on our way to the bikes.

"Oh, I like that," Egon says. "I think I'll get a tattoo that says that. Does Dad do tattoos?"

"No," I say.

"Does Mom?"

"No. I've told you a million times, she's a manicurist and a palmist."

He stares at me and throws one leg over the bike. "So she doesn't do tattoos?"

"No," I say.

"Maybe she should. Hey, maybe *we* should. Hey," he calls back to the shop.

Grampus hobbles out as Meredith goes in and starts picking up. "You guys still here? Come on, you're on the clock, stop eating my money."

"I just had my first business idea. Can we do tattooing here?"

"No," he answers. "But good, keep thinking. See what you can come up with."

"Pro wrestling."

"What?"

"Pro wrestling. We can promote bouts right out there on the grass during the summer when it's nice."

"No big giant monsters tearing up my beautiful lawns."

"Paintball."

"No *weaponry*."

"Skeet shooting."

I think Grampus was on to something there about the juvenile dementia.

"No weaponry. But keep thinking. In my will this is all yours, so I want to see that you can make something of it."

Egon digs his claws so hard into my upper arm that I think he's touching bone. He's a little excited.

"This is ours?" he says.

"No, it's mine. When I'm dead it's yours."

"What about Dad?"

"Your father is a very nice person who wouldn't step on a bug, but I wouldn't trust him to run my model train set."

Grampus has a very nice train set.

"Cool," Egon says. "Thanks, Grampus."

"Don't thank me till I'm dead. Go," he barks, and goes back inside.

What Grampus didn't realize was that we had already accidentally started work on bringing him business by blabbing around school and around town about the magical summer of wealth and boyish wonders that lay ahead of us this summer running our grandfather's golf business. I was pretty excited about it all at first and was perhaps less than careful about shooting off my mouth, but I tailed off considerably once it occurred to me that we might not want all that attention in a situation where everybody else could come and go at will while we were wage-earning sitting ducks, available as the amusement of last resort for every teenager who got bored or restless or cranky with the heat through the long hot summer.

So I shut up.

Egon, you will not be surprised to learn, did not. He told everyone. Friend and foe alike.

"I didn't even realize we had any nemeses, until you told me, Jock," he says as I point them out a block from the barbershop. "I love having them, makes me feel special. I didn't even know what a nemesis was until you made me look it up. Then when I did, I was so excited. That dictionary, it's an amazing thing."

"Yes, it is amazing. I invented it myself."

More amazing, really, were our nemeses, the Noblett brothers. It's just one of those things, and it's like Egon said, we had developed this issue without hardly knowing how. I didn't think I had any problem with these guys, and Egon didn't have any more problem with them than he has with most people.

"I'm misunderstood," Egon pleads.

"You are overly understood," I tell him.

Anyway, at one point there we were, with nemeses. We started having to have some kind of conflict almost every time we saw them. The younger one, Herb, is, like me, going into the high school this year, one year after his brother, Albie. Herb is bigger and stupider than his older brother, but we got through the first seven years of school together without hardly a nod between us, yet once we hit eighth grade it was like he started taking steroid injections or something because he started getting bigger and hairier, the shape of his head started changing to something like a camel's, his eyes were always angry red, and he seemed to think somehow Egon and I were the source of whatever misery he was suffering. It made no sense to me.

"Ya. That, and the one time when I lost his bike in the lake. How was I supposed to know it was his? It was just lying there. Other than that one thing, it makes no sense."

Oh, right. The spokesdevil has a point there.

We approach the barbershop coolly, but confidently. To our credit, I must say we do our part not to stir up trouble with the Nobletts without wimping out at the same time. They are directly across the street from Mom and Dad's place, Fame&Fortune, standing in front of the convenience store with very obviously nothing to do. We don't even acknowledge them as we pass under the old twisty barber pole, leaning our bikes under it before we push the door open.

"Hey, Herb," Albie says, far too loudly to really be talking to Herb, "wanna go for a bike ride?"

"Hey," Egon says to me, "they don't have any bikes."

I stand there in the doorway, my head hanging. We really should get locks, but as there are actually only two people in town who would steal our bikes, buying locks would be a humiliating defeat.

"I know, Egon. I believe they mean *our* bikes."

It should come as no surprise that the next words here are, Egon turns and shouts.

Egon turns and shouts, "Hey, Herbie, I'd let you borrow my bike, but it's too small. Your butt would swallow it."

Herb, I should point out, is no match for Egon intellectually.

That's probably worth repeating, due to its surreal hugeness.

Herb is no match, intellectually, for *Egon*.

"Ya?" Herb shouts. "Like it swallowed *my* bike?"

"Your butt didn't swallow your bike. The lake, which is about the same size, swallowed your bike," Egon says, "and it wasn't my fault."

"Don't worry, guys," Albie calls, "we'll keep an eye on them for you."

"Rats," I say and give in to losing this battle. Humbly, my brother and I get our bikes and wheel them into the barbershop with the Noblett brothers hoo-ing like wolves.

The summer is long. Some people should not be allowed to participate.

Once inside the shop, though, the atmosphere changes dramatically. My parents are so happy to see us, like we're back from a tour in the army overseas. They stop what they are doing—which in my mother's case is nothing—and come right over to greet us.

The kid already in the chair is left stranded.

"Hello, lads," my dad says, "good to see you."

My mother squeezes us both and smells our necks right behind the ear. It's what she does. It's how she meets and greets and senses the state of our well-being. Like dogs do to each other, only more socially acceptable. The hug itself is a mighty thing as she is a powerful woman, much stronger than her husband.

The kid in the chair keeps looking at us all in the mirror.

I alert the barber. "I think he wants a haircut."

"I know," he whispers, "isn't it a pity? I tried to tell him not to do it, but you know how kids are."

"I know," I say, and gently push him back to the haircut.

You probably wonder how on earth my father ever got into the business of cutting people's hair. And you would be right to wonder. For starters there's his own hair, which clearly does not get cut very often. When he comes out of the shower, it hangs straight down to his collar bones, but he almost always has it pulled back tight in a ponytail that makes the top part of his head look the same color and texture as a dolphin's head. If you ask him why he made that career choice he says he decided to *fight the power* from within.

Which means he spends as much time trying to convince people to leave their hair long as he does cutting it shorter. Usually he gets some kind of compromise out of them, which might sound nuts, but people come back to him faithfully throughout the year. I guess they appreciate the personal attention and the fact that he actually cares what they do with their heads.

"How 'bout I stop here?" he says to the kid.

"Little more off the back please, Leonard."

Everybody calls him Leonard. Even tots who have to be raised up in the little fire engine booster seat with the steering wheel call him Leonard. All through growing up, if we tried to call our parents by their heads-of-family titles rather than their names, we got gently reprimanded.

"But that's where that beautiful curl starts," Leonard pleads. "If I cut that, your hair will be straight. This is special, the way it is now. Most people would kill for this bit here. Peach? Peach, would you kill for this curl here?"

Everyone calls my mom Peach. Even if you just met her and weren't introduced, you'd call her Peach. She is kind of peach shaped and peach colored, skin and hair. And her personality is all peach, always. She's total Peach.

"I don't believe in killing, but I would kill a person for that curl," Peach says.

"And the girls will adore this, Peach?"

"They will love it. I'm a girl, and I love it."

Mom is sitting at her station, with Egon across from her. She's using a little tool to clean his fingernails. He's not a huge fan of grooming, but he's a huge fan of this. He's a huge fan of Peach.

"Oh, come on, Leonard," the kid says.

Leonard counters. "I'll charge you a buck less if you let me leave the curl. Now, I'm sure your parents gave you the money, so the extra buck is gravy for you to keep and nobody needs to be the wiser."

The kid is smiling broadly and shaking his head at the singular experience of doing battle with the mad barber. He nods, and my dad whips the protective cloak off him like a matador driving a bull mental. Leonard then dusts the kid off lovingly with that soft neck broom of his, splashes his special stuff on the neck, and lets him out of the chair.

After the kid pays, he returns to the wall of waiting seats as his friend gets up and approaches the big chair.

"You're not here for a haircut," Leonard says disbelievingly.

"I think I am," the kid says.

"Special today," Leonard says, pointing at him. "Every red-haired person gets a free palm reading with every haircut."

"Great," the kid says.

Peach waves Egon out of the chair, sits the boy down, and takes his hand.

"Ooo," she says, "this line here says it is a bad time to get a haircut."

"It says that, really? I have a recital tonight."

"Really, what do you play?"

"French horn."

Peach looks again at the palm, very closely this time.

"Okay, it says maybe a trim will be all right."

Everybody is happy with that, and in short order the kid is in the chair and out of it again, and then I am in it.

"How much money do you chase away in a week doing that stuff, Leonard?" I ask as he pumps up the old chair and brings me up way too high. I've always loved that.

"Exactly, or approximately?"

"Exactly."

"Kind of a lot."

"If that's an exact answer, what would you say if I wanted approximately?"

He steps back from the chair so I can see him fully. He gives me the whole-body shrug. Then he steps up again to start work.

"What are you doing here? You don't need a haircut."

This time he is correct. I like my hair long, over my ears, about to the jawline.

"My boss wants me to look presentable."

"Ah. He would."

"Why is the colonel here, then?" He's pointing with his very sharp scissors in the direction of my brother. "I couldn't cut any hair off him if I wanted to. Jarhead."

"He's here for a professional shave."

"He does *not* need a shave," Peach says, buffing Egon's nails now. "He's just a baby."

Leonard laughs. "He may be your baby, but he's a bristly baby walrus."

"Thanks, Leonard," Egon says. He means it.

"You're welcome, son."

I get just the minimum haircut to look neatened up for my employer, and Egon gets his mustache and sideburns erased in about thirty seconds. When it's time to leave again, Egon hugs Peach, and I try and give Grampus's money to Leonard.

"What are you trying to do?" he says.

"Hey," I say, "if your boss sends you out to get professional, job-related grooming, he should pick up the tab, don't you think?"

Leonard smiles. "I do think. You've got a good

head on your shoulders there, Jock. But I can't take the money. Firstly, because I could never let you pay for anything. Secondly, if my father learns that I took his money for this, he will believe I finally sold out, and that would make him far too happy. I couldn't let that happen. Gotta fight the power, remember that."

I gather it all in. I put the money back in my pocket. "You and your father have a very weird relationship," I say.

"Ya, it's pretty great. You should have seen it when I was in high school. Whew. One time he locked all my shoes in the garage."

The hardware store is about a two-minute trip from the barbershop. We ride down the main street, hang a left at the gas station, and we are there. There is no sign of any enemy combatants, and the store's giant plate-glass front window gives us an easy view of the bikes, so we are relaxed about leaving them there.

Relaxation fades a bit when we go inside and examine our options for vermin eradication. The guy shows us the choices.

"You got your poisons, but I can't sell you those unless you're eighteen. Then you got your tried-and-true, snap-their-heads-off trap. You know when they say, build a better mousetrap and people will beat a path to your door? This is the very thing they are talking about. It's a very fine and effective product."

Egon looks distressed. "I don't want to snap anybody's head off," he says.

This is *very* strange and suspicious. If head-snapping were a regular career choice, Egon would be enlisting.

"Aw," the guy says, "it doesn't ordinarily snap right off. It's just kind of crushed, really."

"Is there blood?"

"Usually."

"No. We don't want that."

This is indeed curious. Egon has never shown any shyness regarding blood. Enthusiasm, yes, shyness, no.

"What's the matter with you?" I ask.

"I don't like it," he says.

"Why?"

"Because, once the mouse gets snapped in there, somebody's got to handle it, with all the mouse blood and all, right?"

"I suppose."

He starts backing away, shaking his head, putting his hands in front of him for protection from whatever, mouse aura, I guess.

"Well, if it's the blood," the guy says, "then you can go with this one. It's glue-based. The little critter gets himself stuck to it, then waits around for you to come and finish him off. Usually there's no blood unless he rips off a leg or something trying to pull loose."

Egon is still walking backward toward the exit.

"I heard there are other traps," I try, "that don't hurt the animals so much. Do you have those?"

"Right, the nicey-nice, bleeding-heart, no-bleeding things. No, but I could order you one. I used to stock them, but people's sympathy for the mice ran thin when they would release them into the wild only to find them right back in the house by the time they got home. And they brought their friends."

"Jock," Egon calls as he goes outside.

"Thanks anyway," I say to the man.

"I have a better idea," Egon says when I reach him, already saddled up.

"What was wrong with those ideas back there?"

"With those ideas, we were going to have to be dealing personally with mice and rats, and their blood and their hair and their bubonic plague like I saw on National Geographic, and have you seen their teeth, even the little ones, like this . . ."

Here he does an effectively scary version of a giant rodent face, using his fingers for fangs.

"You are not supposed to watch National Geographic unless somebody is there with you, Egon. See, this is exactly what happens. Remember when you found out that Tasmanian devils were real, and what they were like?"

"I was out of school for three days."

"Right. Anyway, I guess it's a little late now. What's your idea?"

"My idea is, we put somebody else on the job."

"That's your idea? We're going to hire somebody to work under us? That's not an idea, that's a complete mental collapse. Not only is Grampus not going to let us start hiring our own employees to do the stuff we don't want to do, he'll publicly flog us for being such wimps. Then he'll force us to catch the mice with our bare hands."

Egon has his hands on his hips now, which is serious.

"You are so stupid," he says. "I'm not talking about a human employee, who'll have to be paid all the time. I'm talking about a one-time payment to recruit the natural, historic sworn enemy of the mouse. The cat."

"You want us to get a cat."

"I want us to get a cat. And he can live right there at the complex, working day and night, feeding himself and making sure we never have to get anywhere near bubonic plague."

I give it some thought. It's not the worst idea he's ever had. But that really isn't saying anything at all. He tried once to burn a wart off his foot with a cigarette lighter.

"I don't know, Egon. Grampus said something from the hardware store."

"Grampus also said he wanted us to be bold and decisive and contribute more to the running of things."

This might be the most well thought-out argument he's ever made.

"You *really* don't want to ever touch a rodent."

"Can you not say that word, please?"

I believe we have located my brother's kryptonite.

"So where do we get a cat?" I ask.

"We pass the animal shelter on the way back," he says. "We'll be helping an orphan, saving his life, even. And it'll be cheap."

"Now you're singing Grampus's song."

They only have three cats when we get there. One is missing a leg and an eye and, clearly, the will to live. One has a completely bald head in the space between his ears and shakes like an old washing machine every time you look at him.

The winner, by default as much as anything, is this big yellow-green looking thing with a head nearly the size of mine.

"We'll take him," I say to the attendant.

"Not unless you have an adult with you, I'm afraid."

So I call Fame&Fortune, and fortunately the lovely Peach is only too happy to come and close the deal.

"This is such a sweet thing, boys," she says as we stand in the parking lot, trying to affix a big box of cat to the handlebars of my bike with a bungee cord. "It will be a good thing for you to have a pet to care for, and it will warm up the atmosphere around the golf club. And especially you, Egon, I think a soft furry creature to pet and to love will bring out your caring side, which some people can't quite see but I know is there."

Egon smiles. He is not going to tell her that we

have acquired the services of this soft furry creature as a hit man. But trust me, he is enjoying the irony.

"Are you sure you don't want me to drive him over?" she says again.

"No," I say, getting the box secured tight, "we should handle this ourselves. We're supposed to be responsible."

"And so you are," she says, and is gone.

The cat does not appreciate the ride to work. I can't quite tell if all the bumping around is the rough road throwing the poor cat around or if it's the poor cat throwing himself around out of fury. Either way, it's not a good start to our relationship.

And it doesn't improve things when I place the box on the counter at the pro shop, presenting our surprise with great fanfare, only to have the surprise burst out like a jack-in-the-box with claws and absolutely maul my grandfather/boss.

Cat one, clever creative ideas zero.

5

CROCKERY

When we arrive for work in the morning we are most likely to be greeted by the resident hares. They are big, fast, robust creatures only distantly related to normal rabbits and a lot of them are as tall as Bugs Bunny. They are shooting this way and that all over the course and the driving range and nibbling away at hedges and foliage nearer to the buildings. So it's one of the perks of the job that Egon and I are allowed to hop in the two golf carts and chase them all off to start the day.

It's a disappointment, then, and a bit of a worry, to find both carts missing from their spaces when we get there. Grampus is nowhere around, so we start out on foot through the course to see what we can see.

We get to the par-four third hole, which is over a big hump of a hill, when we see something. About a hundred yards up, the carts are being driven in a wild and reckless manner, one chasing the other in zigzags around the green, nearly banging each other several times. Wiseguy punko types have a powerful attraction to golf carts, and this is what they do with them when they get a chance. But if Grampus sees this vicious abuse of the fleet, he'll have a heart attack.

"Somebody's in for a scuffing," Egon says, barreling down the hill in their direction.

Having a brain that tends to run through the possibilities, I'm a little slower to take off, but I get off my mark and catch up with him.

"What happens if they're huge?" I ask him, jumpety with the bouncing down the hill.

"Hey," he answers, jumpety, "I said somebody's in for a scuffing. I didn't say it wouldn't maybe be us."

There are moments of real lunkhead beauty in my brother, and when he accelerates into the breach with the knowledge that it could be into the jaws of death, that is one of those moments.

It can be hard to sprint a hundred or more yards, all tensed up for battle, all quivery with the unknown, and by the time we do approach the bumper carts near the fifth-hole tee, we are sagging.

So it's probably for the best that the daredevils at the wheels are a couple of laughing old geezoids, with a third riding shotgun.

"Hi, Grampus," I say, wheezing in his direction as he nearly sideswipes me off my feet.

"Hiya, Jocko," he wheezes back.

It's like one of those supposedly scary scenes in a supposedly realistic movie about wild youngsters terrifying good, boring, honest citizens with their motorcycles or hot rods. Egon and I stand there together while first one then the other then the first again of the two carts comes swooping past us at six or six-and-a-half miles per hour, buzzing as close as they can to us, the old dudes laughing insanely as they make the big turn back in our direction again.

Really, it's not a lot scarier than those movies. But the coots-in-cars element gives them the edge.

Their big move is when they come slamming to a halt, almost pinning the two of us between the two front bumpers.

It feels like an hour before they can catch their breath from laughing to talk to us.

"Lads, Jock, Egon," Grampus says to us, "I'd like you to meet the crockery. These two old crocks are two of my oldest and dearest friends in the world. We go all the way back to the marines together. This is Teddy"—he points to the driver of the car he is sitting in—"and this is Lukas. Now, they are our most special guests around here today, so I want you to see to their each and every need—"

Teddy and Lukas interrupt by laughing and barking and squawking some words that sound full of foul old-guy meaning, but fortunately do not sound like words to my ears.

"Right," Grampus says, "make that *almost* their every need. We'll need to stay within budget, after all."

Not that I am in any way an expert in these matters, but it appears to me that Lukas and Teddy's own budgets would not have any limits. They like gold, for starters. I count five bright and chunky rings among their collected nineteen fingers (Teddy is short one ring finger, but has bravely made use of a thumb ring which is either a crucifix or his initial), and the two watches they have on are so serious that even if they are street-corner fakes they probably go for hundreds. They try hard to accent the splash with multi-fruit-colored clothing—lime, watermelon, grape, tangerine—and they have on wraparound shades that are unnecessary for the weather, and if it weren't for all the giggling, the clown outfits would make them look kind of scary.

And they both wear ties. I have never before seen a person wear a tie in the morning on his own free time.

It also occurs to me that these guys do not in any way need my grandfather's hospitality. But I suppose those are the people who always get all the biggest lumps of hospitality thrown at them wherever they go.

"So, which one's mine?" Lukas asks, patting the empty seat in the cart next to him.

I have decided they are a lot more intimidating than motorcycle ruffians. My brother does not share the feeling.

"Pick me," Egon shouts, raising his hand.

"Hop in, Tiger," Lukas calls, waving him over.

Egon hops in and instantly has a dollar bill slapped into his hand. He earns the first tip of the day. The first tip of his life.

It is a life-changing moment for my brother.

"You want to be my grandfather?" Egon asks Lukas.

Loyal as an alley cat, that boy.

Lukas kicks the cart into action, heading for the clubhouse. "Well, I tell you, why don't we take you for a test drive today and see how you work out."

"Yee-hah," Egon says as they head off down the hill.

"Guess that means you're with me, Jock," Teddy says.

I start walking over to the cart, and Grampus slides slowly out of the passenger seat. I'm just passing him, about to climb in, when I catch half a glimpse of his real face, which is peeking out from behind his big-man-on-complex face.

His real face is not so jolly. His real face seems shrunken, with his big boys here.

"Ah, can I meet you down there, Teddy?" I say. "I'll walk down with my grandfather."

"Righto," Teddy says, and takes off after the other vehicle.

"You didn't have to walk me," Grampus says as we walk. "I know the way. I'm not so old yet that I can't find my way around my own golf complex."

"I know that," I say.

Then we don't talk. The sun is just now strong enough to start boiling off the dew from the grass, which is everywhere you can see. If you look right you can see little heated water vapors rising and sunshine tapping individual bubbles on individual waxy blades. The tracks of the tires of the carts have made serpentine designs all over the place and right now even they look like a swirly swooshy part of the grand design of the place, like very fancified musical notes splashed across this gigantic green page.

It really is a beautiful place he's made of it here. You can see why a guy wouldn't mind spending his days here.

"This really is a beautiful place you've made of it here, Grampus."

He has his hands stuck hard into his pockets. The sun is warm enough that the shirt could be coming off him at any second.

"Ah," he says, yanking one hand out of a pocket and gesturing off to the distance, to the future home of the fourteenth hole, where his digger now resides.

Then he's not talking again.

"Ah, what?" I ask.

"I just wish I knew they were coming, is all. Just wish I knew."

He's a different guy. He is a different guy from the one who marched around in the sunshine yesterday, getting his back into groundskeeping and golf teaching and order-barking. He's a different guy for sure from the scrappy happy codger of a little while ago out there cutting loose with his buddies.

He looks like something I have never seen in him before, not for one second of all the time I've known him. He looks embarrassed.

"So what, you didn't know they were coming. Were you running around the course with no clothes on when they got here?"

He lets out a little laugh.

"That would certainly scare off the hares and the seagulls . . . ," he says.

"And the crows and the raccoons and the paying customers," I add.

He takes his hand out of his pocket again just long enough to give me a little clip behind the ear. Then he puts it away again, and with it the smile.

He's shaking his head and looking down at the grass hard, like every inch needs inspecting as we approach the clubhouse.

I don't understand what he's thinking. If this were my place, I'd be strutting around like the rooster in the henhouse. I would *expect* people to envy me, no matter who those people were, if I had my grampus's life.

"So much money," he says, "just so, so much money."

I don't have time to inquire exactly what money he means because he doubles the length of his already lengthy stride, leaving me in his wake as he steams into the clubhouse. I jog and come in a bit behind him, passing the two haphazardly parked vehicles at the door.

Inside, it's like a party. Meredith has arrived to watch over the café and front desk, and the crockery is intrigued. They are leaning close and talking loud to her in a way that says their day has somehow gotten even better already.

Hearing us walk in, Lukas spins and says to Grampus, "This your girlfriend, Gus? You lucky old goat, mine is practically twice her age."

Grampus speaks calmly, through a smile as real as his recently acquired teeth. "Boys, I'd like you to meet my granddaughter, Meredith. She's just graduated high school."

"What?" Teddy says, astonished.

Grampus looks to Meredith, who looks underwhelmed by the attention. "Meredith, why didn't you tell—"

"I did," she says, "but Egon told them I was your

girlfriend, and they liked his story better."

"Listen guys," I cut in, "usually the rule is, if there are two stories and one of them is Egon's, go with the other one."

"Hah," Teddy says, pointing at Lukas, "I told you I got the smart one."

Why am I starting to feel like a racing cockroach with a number on my back?

"Where is our dear brother?" I ask my sister. She points in the direction of the kitchen part of the café.

As I head that way I hear Grampus say to the guys, "Have you seen the rumpus room yet?"

It feels like we've all been sentenced to doofdom when he calls it that.

"Hey," I say when I come up on Egon in the kitchen, pawing at the fridge like a raccoon at the garbage.

"Hey," he says, closing the fridge and turning to face me. He's got a slice of floppy yellow cheese in each hand. He opens wide and takes a mighty chomp of one.

He's struggling with it. First his face crinkles all up, then he pulls the thing back out of his mouth and stares like it has done something vicious to him.

"I think you want to strip that cellophane wrapping off before you eat it," I say.

He peels the wrapping from the cheese. The world is already a brighter place. "What can I do you for?" he says cheerily.

"What do you think of the crockery?" I ask.

"The dudes? My pals? Teddyo and Luka-duka? What do I think? What do you think I think?"

It's kind of become no surprise now what he thinks of them, but I still need him to answer. "Yes, Egon, what do you think?"

"I think they are about the most incredible guys I have ever met. I think they're amazing. I think they are gods. I think I want to hang around with them as much as they'll let me."

"Jeez, Egon, calm thyself, will ya? I'm not at all excited about the idea of hanging around playing flunky to those two all day long."

"Fine," he says, inhaling the second slice of cheese, "don't. I'm flunky enough for both of them. I could flunky for a whole flock of geezers if they acted like these ones. I'm gonna get rich. You know he tipped me twice more since we left you. Once he tipped me just for getting out of the cart."

"Why?" I say. "Did you fart?"

He pauses, then, "That was beside the point. And,

then he tipped me again when I held the door for him on the way into the clubhouse. I'm telling you, Jock, this is the ticket. And if you don't want to do it, I think it might be even better. If I can do stuff for both of them, I might be able to work it into a competitive situation where they keep trying to top each other."

It is with no great pride that I tell you my brother is now flapping his arms and bouncing on his toes with excitement as he spins his vision of paradise.

"By the end of the day I'll be able to buy and sell you," he says in a voice that sounds like he honestly expects me to be happy for him. "How great is that?"

"You're a fine guy, Egon, you know that?"

"Thanks," he says, patting my shoulder as he walks past on his way to his fortune. I detect no sign that his thanks is insincere.

We all gather again in the rumpus room. Grampus and his pals have whipped up a quick game of snooker on the sprawling green-felt table. It is an antique, which Grampus keeps in shape with loving attention that makes it as impressive a green spread as anything out on the course. It is not a coincidence that he has brought them straight in here even though it is way too early in the beautiful day to be hunching over pool with so much else to do. He bought the set at an auction of the estate of a mad old local robber baron who died with no heirs to inherit his stable of live llamas and dead stuffed bison and bears and antique Indian motorcycles and medieval torture equipment. It's a table worthy of showing off to anyone, and Grampus has an almost crazed need to do just that.

And these guys aren't just anyone.

"It's snooker, you know," he says.

"Name your price," Teddy says, with his checkbook already in his hand.

He has made my grandfather's day.

"You can't have it," Grampus says serenely. But I know better, and he's not serene at all. He's winning this duel, and loving it.

"Are you sure you heard the words this man was saying?" Egon says because he cannot possibly comprehend what is unfolding here. "He says you can name your price. That means any figure in the world you—"

"I am aware what it means," Grampus says, smiling. "But of course I could never part with such a thing of beauty. How could I ever replace it? It is one of the centerpieces of the entire complex, and it adds an air of elegance and uniqueness that we could not do without."

"I could do without," Egon insists.

"Then," Teddy says, appearing just as incapable as Egon of understanding my grandfather's position, "name your price, and then triple it."

An involuntary whimper squirts out of Egon as the horror plays out before him. Lukas is by now the only one shooting pool, er, snooker. He's sinking shots from every angle, smiling contentedly at both the shot making and the deal making.

"Now, Teddy," Grampus says, "you are welcome to come here to my place and enjoy this lovely table any time you want. I couldn't possibly sell it, but it would be a pleasure to see you here enjoying it."

I know that is no lie. It's like Grampus cannot enjoy what he has unless someone is telling him how great it is. And if they want what he has, that's the jackpot, the seal of envy.

Teddy smiles a kind of smile I cannot quite identify, maybe because I don't know or understand rich people. But as he tucks his checkbook back into his pocket, the smile seems weirdly built, like it's been hung up there on his face with a hammer and nails.

My grandfather's smile appears far more genuine.

Now is when I beg off the caddy/cabana boy assignment. "If you all don't mind, I have a number of things I wanted to get to around here today, so could Egon tail you around the course? That way the three of you could just take the one cart and leave the other one for other duties."

Grampus looks at me a little funny but not disagreeably.

"Sure," Teddy says. "We don't mind, do we, Lukas?"

"I don't mind," Lukas says, "if Mr. Egon doesn't mind."

"Are you kidding me?" Egon says. "Dingleberry was just going to slow us down, anyway."

Oh, cripes.

"Dingleberry?" Lukas says loudly, laughing with me, of course, and not at me. "Oh, Egon, you are a rascal."

"I am," Egon says. "I'm a rascal, wait till you see . . ."

It's like they've been friends forever. It's like Egon was in the marines with the two of them and not Grampus. At any rate, it suits all parties when they head off for a round of golf and hijinks, leaving the rest of us to the business of running things.

My grandfather gives me a serious nod as he heads for the door himself. Then when he reaches it he turns to look me over again. "I like your work ethic, Jock," he says.

It was more about not wanting to go with that traveling circus, but this is a bonus. If he knew how much I appreciated his rare praise, he might start charging a fee. "Thanks," I say.

"If you finish up all those jobs you need to do, meet me down in the field and you can join in some serious work finishing off that fourteenth hole."

"Sure," I say to him. To myself, I say maybe not. Grampus's "serious work" would break a twenty-mule team.

"What are these important tasks of yours?" Meredith says once he is gone and I am trapped with her. She has taken her comfortable seat behind the counter, opening up her book and waiting for paying customers. Even though I am not bothering her in any way, she is looking over her book at me in a threatening and accusing manner. "I thought you were just the ball boy. Are you just trying to get out of something? Are you just hoping to hang around here and get on my nerves? What could you possibly have to do that's important?"

"Well, for starters, nobody has seen Genghis for a while. I thought I'd look into that."

"What's Genghis?"

"He's our cat."

"We have a cat?"

"Yes, Meredith. He's here to take care of the rodent problem."

"We have a rodent problem?"

"Never mind. Just go back to reading your book."

"Ah, you'd like that, wouldn't you?" She slams the book closed.

"Sheesh," I say, and start my search. She follows me as I walk back through the pro shop, through the rumpus room, into the inside seating area of the café. I half crouch as I look all around for the cat, to see what clever killer spot he has chosen for himself to skulk and pounce and kill.

There is no sign of a cat. There are, possibly, signs of a rodent.

"What are those?" Meredith asks as we go along. She's pointing to small black forms, sunflower seeds, perhaps, or bits of mud fallen off the spikes of some sloppy golfer who has ignored prominent signage saying "No spikes in the clubhouse." That would infuriate my grandfather worse than if it were something else.

"Is that mouse putty?" Meredith says. "What is

mouse putty doing in here?"

She is very loud.

"It's not," I say.

"Then what is it?"

"I don't know. Maybe it's mouse golf balls. It is a golf club after all, Meredith."

She pursues me as I continue the hunt. I'm still hunched over, scanning for the cat, while Meredith is behind me, hunched over, pursuing me for answers. The only thing this train is missing is an engine—a cat, at the front, creeping along after a mouse.

We reach the kitchen.

"I ask you again, why is there mouse putty in here? There didn't used to be mouse *anything* in here. I thought Grampus had you get rid of the one mouse we ever had? Then you went out and got a cat? To kill a mouse after we didn't even have one anymore? Then suddenly we have evidence of mice. Hey, Jock, did you maybe buy a big mouse by mistake?"

Even before she was a college-bound high-school graduate with a gold Honda scooter, my sister talked to me like a half-wit.

"Why don't you go back to work and leave me alone?" I ask. Beg. Pray.

"I like being with you."

When she's bored, she gets sadistic.

"Meredith, please, can you have something like a heart? I'm here on a pest control assignment, I have lost my main weapon in the fight, and I'm making like a buck fifty an hour doing it. Should I really have to put up with being tortured by you at the same time?"

"Really," she says brightly. "One-fifty? He pays me ten times as much as you and I sit there doing practically nothing all day."

It occurs to me that there actually is one cat and one mouse in this room at the moment.

Bing-bing, and somebody up there likes me because the bell rings on the door, indicating that we have a customer.

"Don't miss me too much," Meredith says as she leaves for the front desk. "It must be pretty lonely work, searching for invisible animals."

"They're not invisible," I call at her.

"Why don't you invent *human* imaginaries, like normal friendless saddo boys do?" she shouts back.

Neither the animals nor the friends are invisible. You just can't see either at the moment.

I am on my hands and knees now, trying my hardest to prove it. She is right about there being suspicious pellets around. I trace them to the refrigerator, where they seem to go underneath, as well as around in both directions. And beyond that, along the walls in both directions away from the fridge. I get up off my paws and examine the countertop. There is one path that goes to the microwave, and then continues on to the toaster oven—which amounts to the entirety of our cooking gear.

It's unbelievable. This mouse has the run of the place. It's like he is mocking the authorities, leaving a very visible trail of all his movements the way criminal masterminds leave taunting notes for the cops.

Only the notes don't usually carry bubonic plague.

I am never eating in this place again. I am bringing my lunch. Even when I bring my lunch, I am not eating it here in the indoor part of the café. Even if it's raining, I'll eat outside.

Oh. What if everybody feels this way? Well of course everybody is going to feel this way. Who wants to eat in a café that is frequented by more mice than people? Cats. We could open up the world's first restaurant for cats, there you go, an innovation, just like Grampus wanted.

Grampus. This is going to be bad for business and, so, bad for Grampus.

Speaking of cats, jeez, Genghis, just show your giant head and the mice will flee in horror. You won't even have to work and we'll give you a nice can of tuna fish, ya lazy ripoff of a blob of a furbag.

I grab the little dustbuster off its hook on the wall and chase the trail of black beans all over like I'm using one of those gadgets to find valuable metal nuggets all over a beach.

It occurs to me that if we had more than this little car vac to police things, we might not be in quite this sorry shape, cleanliness-wise.

"Hey there, handsome."

It's Meredith. It's Meredith and it's flattery. Cripes, it can't be good.

"I'm busy cleaning," I say.

"And doing a heck of a job," she says.

"Stop, Meredith, you're scaring me."

I'm not even looking at her as I concentrate on the disgusting little job at hand.

"You're a funny guy."

"What do you want?"

"Yo-ho, Onion Jock," comes the big, happy, confident voice of Carlo, Meredith's boyfriend. He is always happy and confident, which is why I like him, and why I don't.

"Hey, Carlo," I say, turning to them now.

"Cover for me?" Meredith asks. "At the desk?"

"That's what you're being nice to me for?"

"Yes."

I shrug. "Fine."

She comes over and pats me on the head. "You are a good guy. I don't understand why you have no friends."

"Really?" Carlo says. "I'll be his friend, then."

"See?" Meredith chirps. "It's win-win."

Go. Please just go.

They go. I make my way, happily, to the front desk, where I have never yet worked. It will make a nice change from what I was doing, even if I haven't got a clue how to run things.

Bing-bing, the door opens to my first customer.

It's Meredith. "You going to be all right?" she asks, like a regular, decent person with feelings.

"Sure. This is the easiest job in the place."

"Aren't you going to ask me for anything in return? Especially after what I said about the money I make that you don't?"

It hadn't actually occurred to me. Having Meredith scram, having the place to myself, feeling in charge, not playing bathroom attendant to a cocky mouse, all seemed like reward enough.

"I wasn't thinking about money, actually," I say.

She shakes her head. "If the boss heard you say that, he'd have you drug-tested."

"Egon would slap me."

"Thanks, Jock," she says warmly, "I'll get you back."

I flinch at the words. Habit.

She throws me one of those air-kiss things as she backs away from the glass door. Can it get you if it's through glass?

The Honda's engine revs up, and my friend Carlo waves at me as they whip by.

How sad is this? I get a little charge out of the wave he gives me. I guess it is win-win, though the kind of win-win you wouldn't want to tell anybody about.

I like the front desk. I'm on it well into the afternoon, and the pace of things suits me fine. About once every fifteen minutes one or two people come in for the driving range. Driving range is easy. All that happens is I take their money and ask them how many balls they want to hit. In exchange for cash, I give them tokens, which they take over to the ball-dispenser machine, which gives them twenty range-quality balls for each slug. Then I watch them happily trot off with their baskets of balls toward the driving range.

Everybody is happy going to the driving range. They are not always happy when they are on the driving range. I know because I have watched. The serious golfers can go either way, depending on whether they are slicing or hooking, popping them up or driving them on a line. Those guys, even when things are going right, are always a little tense and determined. Doesn't mean they are not having a good time if they are making strides with their long game. It just means it doesn't show up on their grim, serious faces.

The casuals, though, are consistently fun. We get a steady stream of people out on the range who never make it out to an actual golf course and clearly never intend to. These people are happy, for reasons of their own, to stand in a bay and smack the daylights out of a bucket o' balls with only a mild regard for where they land. Some of them find out they aren't bad at it, and eventually we see them progress to actual games of nine or eighteen (or thirteen) holes. For a great many, though, the hitting is the thing. I believe somehow we are providing society a valuable service by giving some of these people something, and someplace, to hit.

Parties of golfers show a little less regularly, but they show. They are good for business because they pay a decent rate, they are numerous, and they make the place look busy—populous and prosperous. I set up two foursomes in my time at the desk, and even though I have to read the prices on the wall just like they do, I pull it off okay.

I even sell a calfskin glove to one guy. It feels like a good day to me.

What it is not, though, is a taxing day. Considering that it is summer, the weather is ideal, the facilities—okay, except maybe for the café—in top shape, there is not what you would call a rush of business. I wonder what it must be like in the winter. I've never come here in the winter. I'm guessing a lot of other people haven't, either.

But for the moment, I have to say, this feels ideal. I am having an ideal day.

And I'm not the only one.

Meredith comes sweeping through the door, and she is alight. It's like light is coming right off her and illuminating every corner of the clubhouse. She vaults the front counter and gives me a kiss on the cheek. She doesn't say a thing, though.

A minute later it's a very different ball game. Egon

and the geezers shove their way in, and if you closed your eyes you could feel like a whole convention of clowns had just burst onto the scene.

"Dingleberry," Egon says, "you are so stupid."

Yes, the mood is festive.

"You should have come with us," he crows. "It was the most hilarious day, the most fun a guy could ever have while being on the job. I want to be these guys' flunky all the time."

"Ya?" I say, mighty and righteous. "Well, they don't pay your salary, Grampus does."

"Pffft," Egon says, and he makes it sound even snottier than you'd think. "That's not pay. *This* is pay."

He holds out his right paw for me to see. Hanging there loosely around the knuckle of the middle finger is a ring. A ring and a half, honestly. It's a big, thick, bright gold ring, with a big bright Indian chief coin set right in the middle of it.

"What are you doing with *that*?" I ask.

Meredith comes over. "Did you steal that, Egon? I mean, *where* did you steal that, Egon?"

"Ah," Teddy says, waving at us with a gesture that looks like it says, "go away, get outta here," but doesn't because he comes up close to talk to us at the same time. "He liked it. He was a great little helper for us today. Time of our lives, had a ball. Lukas, did we have a ball?"

"A ball was had by all," says Lukas.

"See? And the ring was getting too small for me, anyway. Hey, funny thing, isn't it, how everybody blames a ring for getting too small when really the ring stays the same but my fingers keep chubbing out. Started on my middle finger, then transferred to my ring finger, then my pinky . . ."

"Then it transferred to me," Egon says proudly.

"What are you so proud of, ya grub?" I say.

"Oh, that's okay," Teddy says, "he's all right. He's a little excited. He's an excitable boy."

Meredith leans to my ear. "Grandad's going to be an excitable boy if he sees that."

I swallow hard. It doesn't bear thinking about.

"Thank you very much," I say, "but really, we're not allowed to take things from customers."

"What?" Teddy says. "What kind of rule is that? There's no sign. You got a sign for everything here. 'No golf bags on the driving range'; No food on the course'; 'Beware of waterfowl'; 'For a full round pick your favorite five holes and replay them.' But no place does it say you can't give a gift to a good worker."

"I know it's not on a sign . . . yet." I look hard at Egon, who doesn't care. "I'm sure it will be posted soon. My grandfather would not approve of this at all."

"Where is your grandfather, anyway?" Teddy says, looking all around him now. Lukas, who has found himself a seat, starts calling out, "Gus! Hello, Gus, where are you?"

"He's down working," I say. "Down the field with his digger, developing the fourteenth hole."

The two let out small, hard chuckles. "Take us to him, then. We have to see him before we go, thank him for his hospitality. We can sort out the gift problem while we're at it."

I don't get a great feeling from this.

"Hey, Meredith," I say, "since I'm tied up here working the desk . . ."

She slaps me on the shoulder. "You're off duty, bud. You're free to go."

Lucky me, I go. We go. The whole happy lot of us—me, Egon, Lukas, and Teddy. You might almost think we were a real golf foursome as we high-step it across the fairways. But don't.

The other three are laughing and joking like the best of buddies the whole way. As we hit the final downslope to where we can see my grandfather working in his digger just ahead, Egon and Teddy even high-five over something having to do with birdies and bogeys. Their rings clink together like they are making a toast.

He sees us coming. I see him see us, but then he just stares ahead again, working the machine that is working the earth into the shape he needs it to be.

"Gus, Gus old man," Lukas calls when we are all down there circling him like a wagon train. At first Grampus doesn't pay attention, then after a few more muscular scrapes with his digger, he gives us a look.

Teddy waves at him to shut down the machine, and he does.

"We just came down to tell you how much fun we had at your place here," Teddy says. "But obviously not as much fun as you're having."

Grampus laughs and steps down off the digger.

"Ya, clearly you been holding out on us, Gus," Lukas says. "Why didn't you share your best toys with us?"

Grampus keeps laughing along, but as his feet hit the ground I notice his knees buckle a little bit. He catches himself, awkwardly, and as he straightens up, his hair flops over the wrong way.

The wrong way. There is no real right way, but there is a more wrong way. Because my grandfather's one outward visible sign of weakness and insecurity is his comb-over. He has so little fair hair to work with that he has to gather all the hair from around one ear—like a crescent moon stretched across the sky— and connect it with the modest crop on the other side. I don't know how long he has to work on it every day, but it is elaborate the way he gets the tips of the hair from the one side to blend like a perfect solid mass with the ends on the other side. The whole deal is held in place with what can only be the bondo stuff they use to mend car fenders.

It makes me sad nearly every day the first time I see Grampus's comb-over. On the rare occasion when it gets disrupted, it's the sorriest sight in the world.

And he doesn't know it.

He stands there, shirtless, absolutely sprinkling with sweat, and his hard hat of hair standing up like a turtle on its side.

We are never allowed to talk about it. We are not to discuss, mention, or even acknowledge the existence of his comb-over, so even helping him appears to be impossible.

Fortunately, there is outside help.

"Hey, Gus," Lukas shouts. "Your hubcap is popping off."

Oh, no. Even Egon looks worried.

"What?" Grampus asks suspiciously.

Lukas points at the problem. "Your hubcap. Your Frisbee. Seems to have got itself tipped. You might want to close the lid." He even goes to the trouble of miming the open-close motion with his own hand on his own head.

This kills me. This isn't supposed to happen. My grandfather is the kind of man you are supposed to respect. To admire. These little life-jokes are supposed to be played on somebody else.

Grampus has his eyes locked on Lukas as he reaches up and closes his lid. It does, in fact, move and snap into place like it is attached by a hinge.

"Glad you enjoyed yourselves," Grampus says, with a smile and a pop in his voice. He acts as if the incident never happened, and since he has not acknowledged it, we will all act the same.

"We'll surely be back," Teddy says. "Maybe when you get these last five holes dug. Kind of weird, replaying a random five instead of playing through."

"Ya," Grampus says, "well . . ." He gestures a long, glistening leathered arm over the general direction of the still-invisible final holes. "It's coming along."

"You know," Lukas says, "one of my companies, my landscaping division, does a lot of just this sort of thing. I could say the word, and they'd have this thing knocked into—"

"No," Grampus says abruptly, "but thank you, Lukas. I like doing most of the work myself. It's not fancy, but—"

"No, it's not. It's not fancy and it's not finished. Gus, *thirteen*? Thirteen holes? That's not even even. You trying to make golfers dizzy playing your course?"

"What is that on my grandson's finger?" Grampus murmurs.

Egon, I notice, has been silent since we got down into Grampus region, and I know this is why. He's a goon, but he's no dummy when it comes to certain subjects such as his own personal wealth and greed.

"Isn't it incredible?" Egon says, going forth in a brave but doomed attempt. He goes right up to Grampus and waves the ring in front of his face as if to blind him with gold dazzle.

Grampus remains sweaty cool.

"That's, nice, Egon. I bet you enjoyed that. Now they're leaving, so give it back."

"Oh, no," Teddy says, "let the kid keep it. My fingers are all too fat, anyhow. I'm not like you, Gus. I haven't been able to work off all the weight over the years and still stay so hard and strong. You're looking great, by the way. The life suits you, I gotta say. The working suits you. I'm jealous. I wish I still had the knack for all that physical *labor*." The way he says the word and shakes his head, it's as if he is talking about some weird, foreign, slightly seedy trick.

Grampus smiles, nods, and says in an unmistakable tone that even Egon cannot misread, "Give Teddy back his ring, Egon."

Egon's response is so instant, so crisp and exact, it is as if he is a voice-activated cyborg. He spins, walks, removes the ring, and drops it into Teddy's palm. Everybody caught the tone.

"Well, anyway," Teddy says, going up to shake Grampus's dirty hand, "thank you, old man. We will be back really soon."

"Yes, Gus," Lukas says, coming up next and pumping Grampus's hand hard. "We'll let you get back to work now. But," he says as he walks briskly back up the hill, "think about my offer. Give it some thought. I could have a crew here tomorrow."

Egon runs along to escort them up the hill and

earn five-dollar tips for blinking properly and breathing and not falling down.

"Right," Grampus calls, which translates into, *I ain't giving that no thought.*

"And the pool table," Teddy adds, "if you ever need the cash . . . I'll pay top dollar for that magnificent beast. I'll give it a good home."

Grampus is waving now like they are sailing away on a ship to China, "It's a *snooker* table. And it's *got* a good home," he says, not really loud enough for them to hear.

In bed that night, I'm about to drop off to sleep when Egon calls me.

"Hey, Jock," he says, "look."

I roll over and blink a few times, trying to get him in focus from across the room.

He's lying flat on his back in his bed but looking up like at the ceiling. Only he's not looking at the ceiling. He has his hand up in front of him and is examining it from different angles, inviting me to do the same.

He's wearing the big gold ring. He got it back.

"D'ya love me?" he asks. He is right to wonder.

He is not as bad as he sounds. He is not as bad as he sounds.

"Of course I love you, Egon," I say, hoping to offend him deeply. "You are a beautiful person."

"I wasn't talking to you," he says, "I was talking to the ring."

I hear a kiss. Perfect.

6

CRAZY WITH THE HEAT

It's one of those days where it is so hot, time stops. Motion stops, the air stops, birdsong stops, even thought stops, for long stretches of the day. When I snap out of one of those thought-free stretches, I think, hmm, that must be what it feels like to be Egon.

Other than that, I love these days. It can't be hot enough for me. Because I don't care how hot it gets, how intense and oppressive, because it doesn't get to me at all, I feel like I am walking through a still world where only I can move. It might be I love the horrible heat so much because nobody else does.

"Hey, Egon," I say, walking up to him as he takes his turn cleaning the bathroom.

He grunts. He's lying on the floor, making a flimsy job of pretending to scrub. I knew I would find him here because any time the temperature reaches ninety degrees, Egon automatically volunteers to clean the bathroom. He likes the porcelain and tile against his face.

"Isn't it kind of, ah, unpleasant down there?" I ask, reasonably, I think.

"No," he says in a thick, humid drawl. He sounds southern when it's hot. "This is the cleanest spot in the whole complex right now, because I have made sure it is. Do you not smell the piney antiseptic freshness of it?"

It's extra funny to me, because his face is all but pasted to the floor tiles. He really has no stamina at all for this heat.

"Now that you mention it," I say, taking in a deep chestful of it as if I really were in the forest, "it is awfully piney, antiseptic, and fresh."

"Ya, well it wasn't a little while ago. It was gross. There was a sprinkler in here sometime between yesterday afternoon's cleaning and this morning's. I bet it was you. Were you the sprinkler, Jock?"

"I was not the sprinkler."

Egon pretty much makes up his mind about

something before he asks you a question. "Well, it was disgusting. You should be ashamed of yourself, at your age. And I owe you one."

"Fine, owe me. Let's go do something now."

"Are you numb?" He does not even lift his head to have this discussion. "It's a hundred and seventy degrees outside."

"I know, it's amazing."

"Right, amazing, in a boy-this-is-rancid kind of a way. I cannot wait till I am rich enough to never have to work in this heat or any heat. And you can bet that time is coming, Jockey Shorts."

"You don't know what you're talking about. Heat is great. There won't be a lot of business today because it's too hot for all the wimp golfers out there. So let's you and me take advantage of it and have some fun."

"I am having fun, dingleberry. Don't you see me here with my face beside a toilet? It's gotta be better than whatever insanity you have in mind."

I stand there looking down on the sorry sight of him. It's sad in a way, how heat and humidity bleed so much of the evil greatness out of my brother.

"Does that mean you're not coming?"

"That's what it means. Now stop staring at me. You're starting to make me feel funny."

Very sad. I give him a little kick in his lifeless gut before I go. It's like kicking a hot-water bottle.

Grampus is manning the front desk. He has his shirt on, because that's his rule when he's indoors, but I can see in his face he is aching to rip it off. I peek behind the counter, though, and see that he is bare-foot. That's another of his passions, cool feet. He says he can't think straight without cool feet.

He may be thinking straight, but he's not moving in any direction. He's like a statue of a front-desk attendant. His eyes move around to check me as I go here and there, but every other fiber of his body is in full energy-conservation mode.

"This it for you today, Grampus? Hiding out at the desk for once?"

"No chance," he says. "Work to do."

"Work? You mean, like, physical work, outside in the sun?"

"That is what I mean."

Much as I love the conditions as they are, I would not recommend strenuous activity today to anyone, not even my tough-as-turkey-jerky grandfather. Anyway, it's not like it *has* to be done. Nothing here *has* to be done. It's not like he's in homeland security. He's in *golf*. Also, he's the boss. Also, there have been plenty of days when he squired around some ladyfriend or other rather than bust his hump over groundskeeping detail.

"Take the day off, Grampus," I say. "You've earned it."

"No days off. Days off are for losers. Winners get the job done, regardless."

"Can't you win tomorrow?"

"Jock, you work at a thirteen-hole golf course. That isn't right. It's humiliating is what it is. You want people laughing at you? I don't want people laughing at you."

"Sometimes people do laugh at me. But, sometimes I'm funny."

"We need to make money here," he says, even more grimly. "This place needs to be top-class, and we need to bring in some money."

"Can't it be maybe second class, and we have a little more fun?"

"You sound like your father."

"Ya, he's not much into making money, is he?"

"No, he isn't. Don't know where I went wrong with that boy, but he's tragic."

"Well, no disrespect, Grampus, but I'm kind of feeling like money isn't such an important thing, either."

"Then you go someplace and lie down until that feeling passes."

He does believe this. It's not the first time he has said something similar to a claim that money might not be all that important. He considers that kind of thing to be an actual physical, mental disorder that needs to be addressed.

"You should try and be more of a self-starter like your brother."

I am picturing the self-starter face down on the bathroom floor. It makes me uncharitably happy.

"How 'bout I just get out of your way for a while?"

"That would be an acceptable alternative," my grandfather statue replies. "Once your sister finally shows up, I'll be heading down to the field, if you want to come by."

"Okay, Grampus," I say, and head out into the steam.

I even think, for a second, that I hear the day hissing as I step outside, but it turns out to be a cicada. Which is just as good. I like the way cicadas sing about the heat, like I would if I didn't sing a lot worse than bugs do.

I walk down along the path to the first hole, alongside the pond, by the tall nylon fence that separates the driving range from the rest of the world, past the 200-yard sign, past the 250-yard sign, and I stop. I stand, looking from the perspective a perfectly hit drive would have if it was looking back at the guy who hit it, way over there in the driving bay. That ball would be pretty irritated, I imagine. All I can feel, though, is stillness. There is not one person in all those bays waiting to tee up. I spin in the other direction. There is not one fancy-pants linkster to be seen—or, more importantly, heard—over the entire rolling hill and dale niceness of the whole thirteen.

Sweat is just starting to bubble up on my lip, along my sideburn area, across the ridge of my hairline. The sun is crisping my skin in the places where there is no fat cushion underneath to absorb any of it—my forehead, cheekbones, the bridge of my nose.

I cross the course, hole by hole, taking my time. The grass smells fresh cut as always, but it could just as well be asphalt the way the heat just bounces up off of it. Between holes three and thirteen I count a total of two birds passing overhead, and one cloud that looks to be melting. It is like one of those end of the world movies as I pass from the open expanse of empty golf course into the thicket of woods up the hill at the edge of the course that separates Grampus's complex from the whole rest of civilization.

It's about ten degrees cooler in the woods, bringing it down to about ninety-five. There is no life in here, either, but there is evidence of life. This is a popular spot for kids to come at night, a kind of inside-outside structure ideal for slapped-together parties, picnics, and dates, where they can get together with some kind of shelter from the elements and parents but still have the great outdoors at the same time. I find clusters of cans, bottles, and wrappers. Plastic shopping bags. Evidence of a small stupid campfire somebody tried to light. There is a single sneaker, and a torn Cleveland Indians T-shirt, and a broken tennis racket from someone presumably upset to find this was a golf, not tennis, club.

I feel bad, suddenly. I feel like something kind of rotten is going on. They shouldn't be doing this. If they want to come in here they should treat it with some respect, shouldn't they? If they make a mess, they should clean up after themselves, shouldn't they? What kind of people are these?

Part of the problem is me myself. I should be cleaning this up. I have a job, but I'm tooling around here like I'm on a hiking holiday, complaining about the other tourists and their mess. I should be up here with a big garbage bag, and I will be. This will be my responsibility. If Grampus wants us to be building something big and beautiful to be proud of, I may never be much of a businessman, but I can at least keep it in shape.

I actually love the place. In a way I didn't realize before. I feel privileged, lucky, responsible. Every kid everywhere should have at least one summer spent in a place like this doing what I'm doing.

But they'll have to find their own, 'cause this one's taken.

I have my head down as I contemplate my place in my grandfather's kingdom. Court Janitor, Egon would probably say.

I am actually counting the cans on the woods' floor as I startle, and am startled by, Meredith. And Carlo. They have been rolling around together in the pine needles, and none of us noticed me coming along, and boy do I wish at least one of us had.

"Ugh, cripes, you people. This is the most disgusting thing I've come across in these woods, and that's saying something."

Carlo is fairly unfazed. "Hey, Jock," he says.

What can you do? "Hey, Carlo," I say.

Meredith gets to her feet. Her scooter is parked

leaning against a tree a few feet away. They have a bag from Dunkin' Donuts, and a couple of tall paper coffee cups near them.

"Want a doughnut?" she says in a dark, low tone that somehow makes it sound like I am the problem here.

"Aren't you supposed to be working?" I ask her.

"It's no big deal. Nobody is going to be coming in today, anyway."

"Well, Grampus doesn't feel that way. He's keeping himself parked at your spot on the desk waiting for you to show up."

"Why didn't he just have you do it instead of letting you play Woody Wood Sprite up here by yourself, ya little freak?"

"Because I'm not old enough, remember? *You're* the only one who hires me for front desk work."

"Hey," Carlo says, "were you looking for a cat?"

"I was."

"With a great big head?"

"Yes," I say.

"What color?"

"Greenish."

"I saw it, in that field just before you get to the front gate. He was getting beat up something awful by this big bunny."

Right, good, this makes sense. The one time we go out on our own to come up with an idea for the place, all we do is bring home the feline version of Egon—a fearsome physical freak of a character who loves to fight but has a morbid fear of little mice.

"So, basically, nobody around here is doing the job they were brought in to do."

"I am," says Carlo.

Ick. "You have to go now, Carlo," I say in a bold and risky attempt at authority. As it's a first, I'm hoping to have the element of surprise. "And you, Meredith, come on. You're giving me a lift down to the clubhouse so we can get to work."

I don't know if it's my new manly approach, or their guilt over getting caught, but it works. In no time I am on the back of the gold Honda, swerving through trees down the woodsy path to the clubhouse, and sulky Carlo is walking his way home or wherever he spends these long, lazy days not working.

I give him the friend-wave. To my surprise, he gives me one back, and a smile.

Maybe he really is my friend.

"This thing is so unbelievably cool," I say into Meredith's ear. The breeze is blowing my hair back, and blowing her hair into my face. It is a hot breeze, but the motion of it feels nice. The helmets we should be wearing are strapped onto either side of the rear seat, but the short trip through covered woods on private property in the middle of a hot day in the middle of a long summer makes me feel like it is acceptable this one time. Who's it gonna hurt?

Right. As soon as I think that thought, I think, why did you think that thought, dingleberry?

A woodland creature dashes out in front of the scooter, dropping down out of a tree, bouncing, summersaulting, galloping across the path. It happens almost too quick to see, but the creature is long and low and has a head like a green cannonball.

It's definitely too fast for the driver—still a newish driver—to consider her options, so she jerks the front wheel in the direction the cat came from, then, when we start to slide that way, she jerks it back in the other direction.

The two of us and the bike slide to the ground and skid and skip and bounce like three misshaped balls inside a giant, spinning lottery barrel. In the end we come to a rest at the base of three different trees, dust clouds from the parched ground giving the whole scene a kind of dirty heaven haze. Maybe we died. Would we be in heaven this quick? You always think of it as taking a few minutes, at least, to get to heaven. And if it is heaven, the Honda would surely be here, but would my sister?

I'm kind of checking myself, like you do when you have a trauma but no medical training. I'm feeling my ribs, my thighs, my head. I conclude I'm okay.

"I'm okay," I call out.

"Who asked?" Meredith says, already on her feet and rushing to look at the Honda. She crouches beside her prized machine, examining all its parts gently like a paramedic at an accident scene. But she talks to me rather than the patient. "I never once had a crash until you got on the back," she says.

Me. She's blaming me.

"I didn't do anything," I say.

She does not think that fact is admissible evidence on my behalf. She grimly lifts the Honda off the ground, gives it a shake, and declares it roadworthy.

"It's scratched up," she says. She swings a leg over it. This time she puts on her helmet.

I take one step toward the Honda, and she points one long angry finger down the hill toward the clubhouse. Guess I'm walking.

"I was having a pretty good day, before you showed up," she says.

I do not answer. I continue walking down the hill with great dignity, even though the sweat is now mixing with the dry dirt all over me to form an uncomfortable gray paste.

"And if I see that cat-thing of yours again, I won't swerve next time."

The Honda motor starts up and I hear it quickly coming my way.

I continue on the course of great dignity. "His name is Genghis." I will not be intimidated.

It is bearing down on me. I walk.

Honestly? I don't possess this kind of dignity. The mud-sweat is pouring off of my forehead, over my brow, into my eyes like the rapids of a silty river.

I am in the process of turning around to see just as the whirring engine and its rider reach me. I am just in time to catch the outstretched arm, open-palm slap that has been offered to the back of my head but graciously absorbed by my face.

"Aww, Meredith," I squawk, covering one eye with my hand while the other lucky one gets to remain free.

Free to watch as Meredith the inexperienced rider loses her balance before she can get her slapping hand back on the handle, spins out, again, raises a big cloud, again, and wipes out with even more style than the first time.

She's a good thirty feet farther down the path this time, so I suppose it is some kind of progress.

I resume the course of great dignity. But I have to keep rubbing at my eye.

I come to where she has gotten to her feet once more and has attempted to right the poor bike once more. I feel bad for the Honda, which, like me is fairly innocent in all this. Meredith, exhausted now, has crumpled back into a sitting position beside her loyal machine.

I stop in front of them. I extend my hand to her. I must admit being gracious comes fairly easy when somebody flames out so spectacularly.

"I'm sorry," Meredith says, shocking me. "I don't like the heat."

We travel the rest of the way down at a leisurely pace, coasting almost. We park by the entrance and walk in to find Grampus frozen in precisely the pose I left him. It is this I was talking about when I said the heat can defeat time. Grampus is probably not one minute older than when I left him, because of what the heat has done, so heat has done a good thing in preserving him a bit. He could be a 3-D version of the classic old golf legends he has in photographs on all the walls around us.

Being inside makes me feel even more dirt-encrusted and scuffed up. Meredith, who you would think should know better, looks just like some other gnarly eighth-grade boy I just brought along.

"Look what the cat dragged in," Grampus says wearily.

I wave at him, no, no, no cat.

He waves me back, no, no, whatever.

As I approach him, Meredith goes to wash up in the bathroom because she is a girl and because she is the face of the operation whether there is an operation today or not.

I cannot help staring at all the antique players in the antique photos, with their stubby wooden clubs, their big flat caps, their insane shorty pants. They're not even joking about it, either, because they look like serious sportsmen, even the ones who are smiling. They pose, a lot of them in old-styled poses that look stiff even for photos. The greens around them are all gray, or sepia, and where there is sky or sea, it's just different shades of the same stuff. I look back and forth from them to Grampus, from Grampus back to them, and I think I see connections and then just as quick I think the connection is snapped again.

Grampus loves his antiquey photos in their plain frames with glass fronts. I see him, passing by them even when he's busy and just giving them a touch with one or two fingers, just to touch, even when he doesn't have the time to look. He loves especially the ones that show the end of some tournament or another, with a glorious eighteenth behind, a massive mansion of a stone clubhouse, and a smiling golf goofball in front with a monster trophy. "Grampus, do you think that those guys there know that they're in the past? At that moment, in the picture? Because it looks to me like they do know, somehow. But they don't mind. They like it there."

My grandfather turns from where he's looking, which is in the same direction as me at the same pictures. He turns toward me with a slow, mechanical movement like his head is operated by hydraulics. He doesn't suffer fools, or much of anything else, gladly, which I have found from experience of occasional foolishness, so I am prepared for a possible slapdown, heat or no heat. He looks at me for a long lean minute with his face fixed on blank. Then the expression shifts to think-frown, then to a foreign face that does not look like it has ever visited the planet Grampus before. Slowly, with the same hydraulic movement, he turns back toward the row of his sacred photos without speaking.

"Egon won't wake up," Meredith says, coming from the direction of the bathroom, drying her hands on paper towels. "He's just passed out there on the bathroom floor, snorting like a pig, while I'm washing my hands and kicking him. Nothing. I mean, are customers *really* going to want to work around that?"

Grampus is still staring at the photos as he walks around the end of the counter, along that wall of fame, touching all the pictures one by one more deliberately and more reverently than ever. He acts like one of those people who can only walk on the white tiles of a checkerboard floor, or will spend all day sorting jelly beans by color and size and irregularity of shape even though they all really have the exact same flavor, anyway.

"See ya," Meredith says to him. He does not respond.

"See ya later, Grampus," I call.

He stops, turns, looks at me, and points. "Okay," he says, absently but not without some sweetness.

Feels like "see ya later" was some kind of deal, rather than just a "see ya later."

"Want me to come with you?" I ask.

"Not today," he says very clearly, but repeats himself anyway, "not today."

We both watch the old man head off down the fields, sloughing away his shirt as he walks, skipping any protection today, daring the sun to take him on.

"You should probably just take the day off," Meredith says. "Nothing much is going to happen here today. We could at least save him having to pay you for nothing."

I shrug. The day will be just as long and just as hot no matter where I go. And I don't want to take his money for nothing. I head for the door.

"Hey," she calls, and as I turn she gestures toward the bathroom. "You're not leaving without that thing."

I go back to get the thing. He is indeed sleeping away on the bathroom floor. I do the right thing and kick him repeatedly.

He opens his eyes and stares at me as I continue, gently, to prod him.

"Do you know how hot it is, dingleberry?" he surls.

"Gloriously hot."

"That would explain why my skin is stuck here."

"Would you like me to help you up off the floor?"

"Would you like me to help you onto the floor?"

Egon truly does not appreciate the joys of high summer. He's lucky to have me.

"Let's go mountain biking, Egon."

He closes one eye for dramatic effect. "Do you have drain bamage or something from too much sun?"

"I don't believe my drain has suffered any bamage, no."

"Would it like to?"

I leave him right where he is.

"He's all yours," I call to Meredith as I run out the door, hop on my bike, and pedal hard, reopening a sweet sweat that will last all day. His loss.

7
...
VISIONS

I am lying in my bed. It's turning out to be the hottest summer I can remember, and the only part I don't like about it is the sleeping part. Sometimes I sleep, sometimes I don't. Sometimes I'm lying there and the dawn chorus starts and the birds seem happy about it all but I have no idea whether I have been sleeping and dreaming of birds and sweat or if I've just been lying there for hours awake.

I dream lots more in the heat. Unless I'm not really sleeping, in which case I'm just thinking in a weirder fashion than normal.

Grampus is in my head. Him and all his golf-playing buddies. I don't mean Teddy and Lukas and the likes of them who pass through the complex from time to time. I mean all the old-timers in the photos. I see them, very clearly, and I see him right in there with them. Some of them are famous types like Ben Hogan and Bobby Jones, but most of them are just nobody characters who happened to win some regional tournament or other and that's how they got into the pictures and that's how they got onto the walls.

"Jo-ock," I hear a voice calling in a floaty cartoon-spooky voice. "Jo-ock . . ."

I'm lying facedown on my pillow, facing the window, away from Egon's bed. I open my eyes and stare at the big-hand leaves of the great silver maple that practically swamps the window in summer. The window is up, and the heat and humidity of the day are already squeezing through the tiny little holes of the screen.

"Jo-ock," the floaty voice says, "you must go-oh. You must scram out of here. You must go to your grandfather. Your grandfather needs you, now." Then the floaty voice slaps me on the head.

By the time I roll over and look, there is nobody by my bed and Egon is all tucked up.

"I must go," I say, getting up. I go over to Egon's bed and shake it madly.

"Knock it off," Egon snarls.

"Egon," I say, pulling on my shorts, "I had a vision. And a voice told me I must go see Grampus."

He props up on his elbows and stares at me viciously. "This is bad. If you turn out to be dumber than me then we're in trouble."

"I had a vision. A person has to answer a vision."

"It wasn't a vision, it was me. You wouldn't shut up about Grampus so I came over and snapped you out of it."

"No," I say, pulling a T-shirt out of the drawer and letting it slide down over me.

"No?" he says.

"No. I had a vision, and a voice. And I must go. Grampus needs me."

"I think the state hospital needs you, actually, but knock yourself out." He drops his big head down onto his pillow.

"Thank you," I say on my way out. "I'll put in a good word for you with the vision."

"Okeydokey, then."

As it is not yet six A.M., I am fortunate in not having to explain myself to anybody else when I leave. Because really there isn't much in the way of explanation for what I'm up to. Other than the fact that I'm awake for good now, there's no strong reason for me to be out and about.

But I love it. I truly do love being out before anybody is on the street. I'm riding my bike along familiar roads, watching the dew on the lawns already giving up the futile fight against today's heat, and it feels all mine. It feels like I am in charge of absolutely *everything* right now because there is not another soul to say otherwise.

I have to confess it is a superb feeling. I have no desire, really, to be a boss, to be bossing anybody or any thing to do what I say. But at the same time, I do have this powerful desire to be *in charge*, to be *in control* of the life that's right here in front of me.

Is this what everybody is after? In their own way? Because this, I understand. I don't understand the things I see that people seem to want, like money and fame and world domination and that sort of thing. I don't. But if it just means they are after different kinds of this feeling I have right here, riding the streets of my own town on my own bike with nothing in the way of my having exactly the morning I want to have, then I think maybe I can understand anybody.

I hope it's true. I hope everybody who wants all those things is after this same feeling here, because it's just fine.

I'm not going to see my grandfather, of course. Not at this time of the morning. That would be rude, for starters, and he's no fan of rude, and he's not shy about confronting it when he encounters it. I once saw him make my father cry for chewing gum at a funeral. Though it was Leonard's favorite cousin's funeral, so I suppose he might have cried anyway, but still.

But also, who knows what I'd find. Probably he'd be sleeping. But who knows? I've heard old people hardly sleep at all, but wander around their houses in the night like the living dead getting themselves glasses of milk and going to the bathroom. Maybe I'd come across him gumming away at his oatmeal with his teeth sitting right there on the table beside him. Maybe he'd be naked even, since he goes around work with half his clothes off in this weather. Old people are eccentric.

He could be getting up to anything there in the privacy of his own home, so we'll just leave his own home private.

I feel like going to work, anyway.

I've never been here so early before. I've never been here alone before.

That feeling I described earlier? About feeling in charge and in control? Multiply it by fifty and add a parade in my honor and you'll be in the ballpark of how this feels now.

I have my own key to the back door of the club-house, and I use it, but not because I want to spend any more time inside than necessary. I want to get a driver and a bucket of balls because I have an over-powering desire to get out on the driving range and hear the sound of just my lone club whistling through the heavy air and whacking the little ball to anyplace.

As soon as I push my way into the place, I see him, the big mouse/small rat jerk who ruins everything. I'm furious as I see him right in the dead center of the kitchen area floor, not even bothering to skitter around baseboards like a respectful rodent. It's like when we all go home for the night, this becomes his domain and playground, and while that may be perfectly reason-able vermin behavior and I should not be stunned by it, I am anyway. I slam the door and run after him.

Yes, it is stupid. I haven't gone three strides before he has disappeared under a table and under the fridge and into the charmed invisible half-world available only to filthy rotten little hairbags like himself.

I know I'm taking it too personally, but I can't help it. He's like the snake that spoils paradise.

Hmm. Maybe a snake . . .

I get my club, and as I pump the machine with

tokens and hear the balls rumble down and into my basket, my mood goes right back up. People make a lot of claims for the magic of this game, and maybe they're not all hooey.

From the first swing I feel like I'm king. There is no one in bay four next to me, or in bay six shooting rockets into the distance to remind me I'm just me. I don't even look up most of the time to follow the balls, because the feel is the thing, and they all feel incredible. In fact, the only times I do find myself looking up are between shots, when I hear one of our many seagulls or starlings yelling at me in the distance and I just stop to listen and to take his advice. Keep your head down. Keep your feet planted. Left arm straight. Follow through.

We have good birds here. Knowledgeable birds, and generous.

"You could be half decent at this."

I nearly leap right off the platform and into the grass where the sign specifically tells me not to go. But I turn to see my grandfather watching from about four feet behind me. "Goodness," he says in a dreamy, quietly excited way, "wouldn't that be something. If you got very good at golf. I mean, really, really, top-flight good. My word, how wonderful a life that would be."

I'm still breathing heavily from the shock. "How

long have you been here, Grampus?"

"Here?" He points at the spot beneath his feet. "About ten strokes."

His eyes are very watery-looking to me. He has his plaid bowling-style shirt on him still, but he's worked halfway down the buttons already. I know he's had too much sun lately, but you cannot talk him out of it, and at the same time he looks like he's been donating blood every day for a year. He manages a freaky combination of over-tanned and anemic.

"Why are you here?"

"Because this is my place. Why are you here?"

"Because I'm hitting some balls."

"There, now that that's out of the way, let's talk about your game."

My game? Do I have a *game*?

"I'm just having fun, Grampus."

"No, I think there's more here than that. I've seen a fair few golfers in my time, and I believe you have something. Your approach, your balance, your mechanics are all very sound for a kid who's never had a lesson before. You never have had a lesson, have you?"

"Nope."

"Well, we'll get that taken care of. But just think about it, Jock. Think, what a life that could be for you.

It's a beautiful life, it really is. And if you got to be great, that could also spill over on us here. You could be the club pro here someday. You could make this a real destination, a place people would travel to come to. I would be so proud of you."

Are there conversations that can fill you with pride and excitement and depress you at the same time? I wouldn't have thought so before this.

"Thanks, Grampus, but really I think maybe you're seeing more here than there actually is."

"That's defeatist, Jock. The worst thing to be in life is defeatist because that means you beat yourself. There is honor in losing out to the better man, provided you lose with strength and class. But there is no honor in defeating yourself. Remember that."

"I will, Grampus."

"Now, don't let me get in your way here. You go back to hitting away. I have to get back to the workshop. I'm very, very close on something now that I think is going to be the next big thing for all of us."

"An invention? You're working on your inventions right now? How long have you been here already?"

He gestures for me to address the ball I have teed up rather than him. "You just attend to your own destiny there, champ. I have to find extra hours for the workshop because the complex is taking up too much time just now. And they both must move ahead."

He's walking away before he finishes talking, so I address the ball.

"And Jock," he says, just as I go into my backswing.

I turn my head, leaving the driver raised over my shoulder.

"I'm very impressed with you, son," he says, pointing at me. "Your work, your way. I feel good about things with you. You're a good kid, and with just a little more motivation and confidence . . . who knows?"

He's not a gushy guy, this guy, so it gives me a little quake. He also wouldn't prefer a regular thank you, so I turn, address the ball, and give it a mighty stroke.

I practically throw myself out into the field with the force of the swing, I top the ball miserably, and for all that, it splurts a very sad few feet in front of me.

"Hitting well is more important than hitting hard," he says as he walks off.

He is very impressed with me, though. All the wondrous stuff happens when you get up real early.

By the time anyone else shows up and we reach normal opening time, I have had a fairly busy day. I have chased away the hares and the seagulls, as much for sport and exercise as for accomplishing anything. I have driven the golf cart around with Grampus's famous trailer contraption, collecting the golf balls from all over the driving range and feeding them back into the machine ready for the next bunch of happy whackers. I have had myself a nice little microwaved breakfast burrito—*after* cleaning up all the little villain's tiny black bullets. I even went around the pro shop and reception area with a chamois, dusting and buffing every surface, every set of discount clubs, every wall picture, until the place was as bright inside as it was outside. When real opening time approached, I took myself out to the group of five circular outdoor tables that make up our open-air dining experience. Each table has its own broad umbrella planted in the middle of it to ward off the rain or the sun, but I feel no need to ward off anything. I plunk myself down on one seat, put my feet up on another seat, and face the general direction of the sun.

As I look down at the table, I notice, not for the first time, the menu, laminated and fixed permanently to the surface so you cannot miss it. Not the menu of eats, but the menu of what we can offer you here at the complex by way of sporting pleasure.

GOLF COURSE

- Par 3 Course
- Adult Round, 9/18 Holes
- Junior and Senior
  Citizen Round, 9/18
- Day Ticket,
  Adult/Junior-Senior
- Club Rental
- Trolley Rental
- Cart Rental

DRIVING RANGE

- 13 Bay Floodlit &
  2 Outside Bays
- 20-Ball, 40-Ball, 60-Ball,
  100-Ball Buckets
- Range open from 10 a.m.,
  Last Balls Half Hour Before Sunset.

GOLF ACADEMY

- PGA Professional Arranged
- One-Hour Lesson,
  Half-Hour Lesson
- Discounted Junior Lessons
- Video Coaching
- On-Course Lesson

GROUPS

- Ladies' Days Discount
  (Selected Wednesdays)
- Over 50s
  (the other Wednesdays)
- Learn Golf in a Week
- Junior Groups
- Young Masters
  Golf Learning Center
- Junior Classes
  Tuesdays and Sundays
- School Holiday Junior Days
  & Golf Tournaments

· SHOP OPENING TIMES ·

Mon.–Fri. 10 a.m.–9 p.m., Sat.–Sun. 10 a.m.–7 p.m.

- Well-stocked Pro Shop
- Light Refreshments Available
- Indoor and Outdoor Sitting Area
- Games Room With Classic Snooker Table

And there it is. It's not like I haven't seen this before because I have, zillions of times. But I suppose it's a bad-with-the-good kind of arrangement where if you're going to get all the fun and coolness of seeing and feeling everything great in that special morning light, you might have to likewise brace yourself for seeing some sad stuff in a way you didn't before.

The menu of stuff looks so sad to me right now. I guess because I have seen so much of how nobody uses any of it. I mean, smatterings come to the driving range; the course itself gets a certain amount of traffic when conditions are just right. But the rest of it? The variety of offerings that make it look like this is a buzzing, happening center of sporting fun and classy country club culture?

That's a fantasy that exists on the menu and nowhere else. Why isn't it better than this? It's a good place. Grampus is a good man, with a good plan and a dream that isn't so big that the world shouldn't just let it happen. This place, this little world, is very much like paradise and I just can't stand or understand people not beating down the doors to join in. You'd have to be nuts not to see the greatness here.

And it makes me so sad I almost don't want to be here. In fact, I don't.

As soon as I hear Meredith's Honda buzzing down the lane, I jump on my bike and pedal away. I just wave as I approach her, and I speed up as she slows down.

You shouldn't feel sorry for a man like Grampus. He's too tough. And he would hate it. And he has the kind of life anybody with a whole working brain would be happy to have.

Does he know that?

You can't ask a guy like Grampus, though. You've already messed things up just by asking him if he knows how good he has it, because he won't like the idea that you even had to ask him. He would wonder what was wrong with him that made you question his spot at the top of his kingdom. The insult is in the question.

In fact, I feel like a dope as I pedal my way, exhausted, back to the complex. In fact, I feel like I have badly let him down, the guy who told me just this morning how he's impressed with me and with my way. So what if we're not crowded? We're great, anyway.

"Where you been, chumpy?" Egon says, greeting me outside the door as if he has been making the whole world spin in my absence. Even though I left him nearly nothing to do and he's probably been doing exactly that brilliantly.

"I went out to play golf," I say.

But there's no fooling my brother. "We have golf right here," he insists, pointing an accusing finger at me.

"Sorry. Did I say golf? I meant polo."

"Well, while you were out playing whatever you were playing at, things got very complicated around here."

"Why? Somebody ask you to recite times tables or something?"

"No, funny guy. Come and see this."

I follow Egon into the pro shop and I have to say it is a sight. Meredith has her arms folded and is shaking her head in disbelief at the people she is attending to.

My parents. Leonard and Peach are here to play golf. I've never seen them play golf, and as far as I know it has never happened before. But as with most things that involve the two of them, when something does happen, it happens flamboyantly.

I think they are aiming for a 1930s style of golf look, distantly related to some of the wall photos where everybody has on a silly hat and doofus pants.

Only my parents manage not to look quite as professional, serious-minded, or monochrome as those people. They have, actually, managed to come up with a crossbreed look mingling the '30s and the '60s, getting the styles of the early days blended up with the candy colors and spacey patterns of the flower-power days.

They look like Bonnie and Clyde got into the dress-up box.

"There he is," Peach says, coming over and giving me a big hug.

"That's right, here he is," Egon says. "Now you'll be in trouble. Jock, make them go away."

Peach just laughs at him, though he is very serious. She has on big lime green satin shorts, kind of like the style boxers wear, a white T-shirt, and a canary yellow vest with textured white daisies all over it.

"You look sporty," I say to her.

"Stop that," Egon says. "She'll think we approve."

Leonard gives me a salute bon-voyage wave like he's piloting a riverboat. He has on a hat that looks very much like a baby blue Frisbee with a pink grapefruit on top, pinstripe baseball pants that stop at the knee, and a billowy shirt that looks like he made it himself out of a spare Brazilian flag he had lying around.

"Well, what do you think?" he asks once he has his partner tight by his side and they strike a pose. "Do we look the part, or what?"

"You look the part of a horse," Egon says. "Would you like to know which part?"

"Bug off, you," Meredith says to Egon. "I think they look adorable."

"Ya," I say, secure in the knowledge that nobody we know is likely to come by and see this today, "you guys look like a million."

They are beaming. I will say this about my parents. You don't have to put a ton of effort into pleasing them. They are, more than anybody I have known, always ready to be happy.

"Thanks a lot," Egon says, "now they're gonna go around looking like that all the time."

It seems like they are waiting for somebody to take their picture, but since there are no cameras around, I figure I should move things along.

"How come you guys are here, anyway?" I ask. "What about the shop?"

"We're playing hooky," Peach says cheerfully. "We just decided, after a couple of hours passed and nobody came in, that we would shut down and come out and play."

"Today," Leonard announces solemnly, "is a day no hairs will die."

"Speaking of hares," Peach says, "was that your cat I saw getting kicked around in the field?"

Sheesh. We're going to have to mount an operation to capture the cat, before he shames the whole operation.

"Okay, we want to get started," Leonard says, clapping his hands. "And we haven't got a clue how to go about it."

"Well, you're in luck," Meredith says. "We have a top staff here to show you along every step of the way."

Egon spins toward the door, stiff and unnatural as one of those little plastic tabletop hockey men. He walks with tiny little steps as if nobody will notice him.

"What are you up to, Jock?" Meredith asks me.

"I was going to go down and help Grampus finish up the fourteenth hole," I say.

"Right. Egon," she calls just as he gets one paw on the door handle.

"Egon gone," Egon says in some vaguely Eastern European accent. "E gone and E no coming back."

"E staying right here to help these nice people or

else E no getting paid," Meredith says.

I'm thinking it's good there are only blood relatives witnessing our performance here.

Egon comes back muttering, "The only customers we get in two days, and it has to be these guys."

Meredith hands a couple of drivers and some tokens over the counter as Peach wraps my brother up, lifting him right off his feet. He's taller than she is, and they are about equally stout, so it's a pretty decent feat. He cannot be surly enough for her. She finds it irresistible. "This is going to be so much fun," she says into his ear before kissing it loudly right in the earhole.

"Ow, Peach," Egon says, "it sounds like a tree falling inside my head when you do that."

"Just start them out on the driving range, getting them used to striking a ball. Then when they've got the hang of it, you can escort them around the course for a full game. We'll find them a set of clubs to use, and you can be their caddy."

"Ooo, you'll be our caddy," Peach squeals at Egon, big-kissing the ear again.

"Ow, *Peach*!"

I can hear them all the way down as I walk to

meet Grampus. Leonard and Peach are cackling away at everything, and Egon is moaning and complaining, two situations that go together perfectly. They love to tease and wind him up, and the more they enjoy it the more wound up he gets, and the more wound up he gets the more they enjoy it. Combine this with the fact that my parents are almost as enthusiastic as I am about the scorching sun, and Egon, as we know, feels somewhat differently about it, and it just gets better. It's an ideal world, and even hearing it from a distance is putting a smile on my face.

Grampus, by the time I reach him, does not appear to be having the same kind of fun. Maybe if his digger weren't grinding away at the job, blocking out the joyous sounds of my family being eccentric on the driving range.

Though somehow I don't think that's it. He sees me coming, and stops the machine moving about. When he stops, he slumps forward, his shoulders practically reaching around to touch each other in the front. He looks wasted. Then he cuts the engine as I reach him. I climb up to his window and hang off the side of the machine.

The hilarity in the distance becomes more obvious now.

"What in the world is that?" he asks.

"Customers," I say.

"Really? Our customers don't usually sound like that."

"That's because our customers aren't usually Leonard and Peach."

"You're joking," he says.

"Listen for yourself."

He does. He puts his ear to the air, and it is a truly remarkable thing. My father and mother, for all the golfing they must be doing, are getting a workout of major intensity just by producing all that racket. The sound of them, laughing, hooting, howling—undoubtedly at the lameness of every shot they make—comes rolling over the hills as if they were being piped over a big concert sound system. It's fair to say nobody ever found the game of golf this funny before.

"What is *wrong* with those two?" Grampus says sternly.

"Doesn't sound like there's too much wrong with them right now."

"Well there's everything wrong with them. You hear that sound?"

"The sound of laughter?"

"That's the sound of insanity you're listening to.

That barbershop of your father's doesn't make any money as it is. And the palm reading and *aroma*therapy (he pronounces it as if he believes the very notion of scent is a hoax) and whatever other hocus-pocus they come up with will never amount to much, either. But it is what they do and all they have, and look, as soon as the sun comes out the two of them shut down the operation and take a day at the beach."

"At least they're taking a day at your beach," I say, gesturing around at what is shaping up to be the legendary long-awaited fourteenth hole. For the first time, it's not hard to see what it is. The old man has actually done quite a number down here. It's about a 200-yard gentle downhill approach, landing here in the area that will be the green but right now is mostly brown. Grampus has used his digger to move earth here and there and back again the way we used to do at the real beach with our very unreal dump trucks and front-end loaders. He's made some nice tricky little rolls leading up to the plateau of the putting area. Off to one side, about twenty yards right of the hole, is a long stretch of sand trap, directly opposite a still-empty water hazard about thirty yards off the other side. Stacked like a row of giant rolling pins in the middle of it all are the rolls of fine turf he's going to lay as a blanket to the whole project.

"This looks great, Grampus," I say. "When is it going to be time to lay the turf?"

"Now," he says. "At this point all I was doing was shaving a little off of one hill, flattening out another bit there. Just carving and shaping really, trying to make it perfect."

"Well, it's perfect," I say.

"It was probably perfect a week ago," he says. "Probably just wasted time and money these last several days, fool that I am."

"Is it really foolish," I say, trying to impress him with my homespun philosophy, "to try and make something perfect and beautiful?"

He looks at me like I've just suggested he turn the place into a bird sanctuary and donate it to the Audubon Society. "Of course it is, if it doesn't make financial sense."

It's the kind of remark that makes you do a double take to check and see if the person's joking. Except two things with my grandfather: one is that it is just the kind of thing he would tend to believe; the other is that even if he thinks something is funny his face never tells.

"Well, Grampus, I believe it's a really fine creation. Whether it took a few extra days and dollars, it was worth it."

He gives me the Audubon stare again. "Why aren't you practicing your golf?" he says.

"*My* golf? I'm in charge of an entire sport now?"

"You might be, if you work at it. Why aren't you at it now?"

"Because I'm working. I'm working for you, remember?"

"Then your job is to go up and play some golf."

"I'd rather be down here with you, laying some turf."

"That's not for you to do. Go on, now."

"Come on, Grampus, you shouldn't be doing all this on your own."

"Are you saying I can't do it? I'm too old?"

If you could hear the tone of him . . .

"I just want to help, that's all."

"You want to help? Make an old man happy . . ."

Sure, it's okay if *he* says it.

". . . by permitting me to dream about you winning the US Open."

"That doesn't get the fourteenth hole built. Or the fifteenth. Or . . ."

"Fine, send Egon down here to help me. You golf, and I will let Egon help me."

"Okay," I say, knowing that Egon would gladly hand-wash my underwear if it meant getting off the job he was on.

It's gone quiet again by the time I hike back to the clubhouse. There are still no other customers, and Bonnie and Clyde seem to have gone underground. I find Egon slumped at one of the outdoor lunch tables, sipping a root beer.

"What did you do," I ask, "club them into submission?"

"No need," he says. "They fired me."

"Fired you?" I laugh. My parents once had a lady hairdresser working at the shop. She was about seventy-five years old, only did three people's hair in six months—and all three of them were her daughter so she didn't charge—and the only reason they fired *her* was that she died.

"Ya. They said I was a drag."

"Were you a drag?"

"I was certainly trying to be. So they said they had learned enough and wanted to head out on the golf course without me. I said fine and held out my hand. I said it is customary to tip your caddy. They laughed and laughed. Then they said they would play nine holes and come back for something to eat, that it would be nice if I could prepare them something from our vegetarian selection. I said fine."

"We don't have a vegetarian selection," I point out.

He holds up his can to me. "I don't believe this has any meat in it." Then he slurps down the remains of the vegetarian selection.

"Well, you're in luck," I say. "You have been rehired. To work with Grampus finishing up the fourteenth hole."

He rests the empty can on the table, and rests his chin on the can as he looks up at me forlornly. "Isn't that in the sun?" he asks.

"Yes, it is," I say. "And don't make your grandfather do any more of that work on his own, ya rat. Get down there."

He stands up, takes exactly one step in the direction of Grampus. "And what are you going to be doing?" he asks in a hostile tone.

If it were anyone else I would lie, or at least feel a little bit embarrassed. However . . .

"I'll be working on my game."

The devil voice, extra crispy in the sun. "On . . . your . . . *what*?"

"My game. Grampus thinks I've got potential. Thinks I could go a long way in the game. Get to be club pro here and everything. So it turns out a big part of my job around here is going to be to play golf and get really good. Cool, huh?"

You know those lizards that can spit poison out of their eyes? My brother is one of those.

"You are making that up. You are making that up and for that you are going to die. Unless it turns out to be true, and then for that you are going to die."

"It's true. And it's all because of my vision I had this morning. You remember my vision?"

"It was not a vision," he growls, "it was me."

"Right, it was my vision that told me I had to go see Grampus at the crack of dawn this morning. And it was when I did that that Grampus saw my gift. I'm gifted now. It was like a religious thing, Egon, and it's going to wind up changing everybody's life."

"Hey, I know how to change your life with a golf club and it won't take any practice at all."

It's working out even better than I had hoped. If I never make the PGA tour, this will be the finest moment in my golfing career. Even if I do make the tour, this will probably be my finest moment.

"Be nice to me Egon, or when I make it I won't let

you be my flunky. Wouldn't you like to be my flunky? I'll tip you if you caddy for me."

He is rumbling with rage now, just a low muffled noise coming off him as he shakes like his engine is idling rough. Finally he turns and starts marching off.

"Pace yourself now," I say, "that's a long walk in the sun for someone like you who is not an athlete like someone like me."

He does not answer. Well, he does but not in words. He turns the corner around the edge of the building, and the next thing I see is him, in a golf cart, putting his way up the hill, shaking a fist at me as he goes.

"Good," Meredith says as I walk in. She hops right around the corner and grabs her helmet off a chair. "Watch the store for a little bit."

"Why?" I ask.

"I have to run out and . . . get some vegetarian options for lunch. Right. Thanks. Won't be long. See ya."

I don't even get a chance to say *I don't believe you* before I hear her scooter zooming out of the lot. Her sudden dedication to the veggie cause is deeply suspicious.

Not that I care. I sure don't feel like playing golf. I

put my feet up on a low shelf behind the counter, fold my hands in my lap, and suddenly realize how early I got up today.

My head is bobbing forward, my chin poking my chest, when Meredith comes sweeping back through the door. There is fresh drool leaking out of the corner of my mouth and laminating half my chin, so I estimate I've been out about ten minutes.

She is flushed, creases of distress zigzagging all over her face. She still has her helmet on. "I'll have my post back, thank you," she says.

"What's wrong?"

She throws herself into her chair. "I . . . up in the woods . . . back at the clearing . . ."

"Jeez, Meredith, again?" I say, disgusted.

"No, it's worse than you think. I ran into . . . Leonard and Peach."

"Oh . . . oh, no," I say, then when I have a chance to think, add, "oh, oh my . . ."

The two of us hang there, traumatized.

"You can take off your helmet now," I say after a while.

"No, I can't," she says, folding her arms defensively. "I might never take it off."

8

DRAIN BAMAGE

The only thing both my father and my grandfather do the same with their businesses is they both run an "Employee of the Month" program.

However, since Grampus believes in it as a bona fide workforce motivator and my father's version consists of a cork bulletin board on which he adds a new picture of my mother every month, you'd have to say they're really two different programs.

I am named "Employee of the Month" for July at the complex.

And in a stunning result, Peach captures the award over at Fame&Fortune.

She gets a lovely new photo on the wall, in her

Bonnie and Clyde golf gear.

I get a brand sparkling new set of fairly expensive golf clubs. I thought I would get maybe a baseball cap or something.

I sense my brother's unhappiness with events when I find my three-iron bent at the same angle as an archer's bow.

"This wouldn't happen to have anything to do with you, would it?" I ask him.

"Hmm," he says thoughtfully, "maybe Grampus thinks you also have the skills for professional archery."

"Hmm," I say, "times like this, I wish I did."

Fortunately or not, coincidently or not, there is more to it.

"Hi, I'm Don Monty. You must be Jock."

Don Monty is the more part. He is the golf pro who gives lessons by appointment here, and he has been engaged to have an appointment with me. He is about six-foot-five, and no matter what angle you get he looks like he's hitting one of those poses model-men strike in catalogues.

"Yes," my spokesdevil answers, "this is the Onion. Hey, do you know Tiger Woods?"

"Not personally, no."

"If you're a pro, how can you not know Tiger Woods? He's a pro too, you know."

"That much I'm aware of. There are quite a few pros. It's hard to know all of them."

"Right, so if you could know any, you should pick Tiger Woods. That's who I would pick. So, what pros do you know?"

"Well, I met Davis Love the third a couple of times."

"Davis *Love*? The *third*? Not even the first string? Are you a real pro? Could we see some identification, please?"

Don Monty points a very long finger at my brother. "Right, you must be Egon. Your grandfather warned . . . told me about you."

"See," Egon says, and rips the golf bag right out of my hands. "I knew there was a mistake. He's here to train me, not you."

I rip it back. "Excuse me, but you forget that I am the one with the touch, remember? And I am the one who is Employee of the Month, with the beautiful Employee of the Month golf clubs."

"Oh, but excuse me," he says and leans close, "but you forget this." He bops me on the forehead with a flat palm.

"No, no, I didn't forget," I say, and draw the already bent three-iron like a sword out of the Employee of the Month bag.

Egon is bouncing from side to side, fists clenched, satanic grin across his face, looking forward to this. I'm waving the club in his direction.

I realize we are putting on this show in front of a very expensive golf pro.

I look up—and up—at him. His mouth hangs open for a second, then he calmly informs me, "We have fifty-four minutes left."

"Egon," I say, "Grampus says you are on weeding and ball-collecting duty. Go do the ball-collecting while I'm having my lesson."

"We don't have any balls to collect," Egon declares.

"We have balls everywhere on the driving range."

"Oh, the *driving* range . . ."

Don Monty keeps listening, shaking his head, checking his watch, "We have fifty-two minutes . . ."

"Sorry, Don," I say, "he's just jealous because I'm the gifted one and he's just the grunt around here."

"I'll give you a grunt . . ."

Don Monty ushers me right out and down to the first tee. He takes the basics for granted, since I do work at a golf course and my grandfather has notified him that I'm some kind of golfing genius. So as I tee it up to start the get-to-know-ya game with my own personal pro, he doesn't give me so much as a hint what to do.

"Okay, prodigy," he says, " let's see the show."

Jeez, I think, that's not very helpful. Especially for someone who's getting paid to make me better. The pressure feels real now, as I go into my backswing, try to remember all the things at once—head down, feet planted, left arm straight, bend left knee slightly, I said head *down*, follow through—and lay into that ball like the prodigy I am.

I won't tell you how that first shot went. How 'bout I just tell you what Don Monty says?

He says, "You can take some comfort, Jock, in the fact that it's not really possible to hit a ball any worse than that unless you miss it completely, and even that might not be worse. So things can only get better from here."

Don Monty turns out to be very wrong. In fact, it's not really possible to be much more wrong about something than he is about how badly I can hit a ball.

It takes me thirty-seven strokes to get through the first three holes. Par for this course would have been nine strokes. Don Monty goes from observing me and not giving me any pointers, to giving me two or three pointers every time I address the ball, to actually helping me swing the club. By the time I finally sink the second hole he has run out of tips and has gone back to saying nothing. By the time I am 280 yards from the third hole (and you are only 220 yards from it when you *start* the third), he has regressed to making *remarks*.

My golf instructor is so offended, he is heckling me.

"Maybe if you try hitting with the other end of the club," he says.

Once I figure out that these are no longer, in fact, genuine suggestions, I try and make the best out of the situation. I figure a top-class athlete has to withstand great stress and pressure, so I go quietly about my business.

"Has your grandfather actually seen you play?"

"Yes."

"Golf?"

I really have to stop answering.

"I'm going to have to get more money for this, because by the time we finish the round you'll be too old for the junior's rate."

You know what? I don't care. Everything he says

just makes me more determined. I can do this, and I will do this. My grandfather has faith in me and that is what matters. He is investing in me and counting on me and it really would be incredible if I could make something out of myself with this game and do my Grampus some good. Do us all some good.

I press harder. I concentrate more. I focus. I hit chip shots and wedge shots and one-irons and five-irons, and my fundamentals are in my mind the whole time. Once I even try the bent three-iron to see if that helps. I miss the ball completely and try the four.

And it seems like every shot gets me just a little closer.

To oblivion. From where I am now, in a small grove of trees downhill from hole number three, I cannot even see the flag I am supposed to be aiming at.

Doesn't matter. I bend my knees slightly, keep my head down, and swing away in what is probably the right direction.

The ball travels straight and fast and feels like the sweetest shot of an admittedly not very sweet day.

The ball hits a tree dead center and bounces back, to me, then past me on its way back to where I was three shots ago.

"Are you traveling backward in time," my coach

asks, "so you can still get the junior discount? *Ouch!*"

The ouch is something I have to turn around for. I do, and see Don Monty rubbing the side of his head and looking around. About ten yards away parked by a tree, is Egon. He has a bucket o' balls. He's taking them out one by one like he's pitching batting practice, and he's pelting Don Monty.

"Leave him alone," Egon says, firing another ball right off Don's head. As you can imagine, he's very good at this sort of thing.

"I'm sorry," Don says, holding up his hands in a surrender. He appears genuinely sorry, the way you are when you get caught at something and only the presence of a witness wakes you up. "But he really is hopeless."

Maybe he's not that sorry.

"I know he is," Egon says, then as Don Monty drops his hands, lets fly with a hummer of a throw that catches the big smug lug right in the throat. It sounds like a foul ball as it deflects off the prominent Don Monty Adam's apple.

"Right," Don Monty croaks as he holds his throat with both hands. It looks and sounds as if he is trying to strangle himself. "Time's up now, anyway."

He stumbles away, muttering something about working on my driving.

"Oh," Egon calls after him, chucking one more ball that plunks him in the back, "you're a *driving* instructor, that was the confusion . . ."

Egon turns back to me, smiling. He likes doing stuff like that.

"Thanks," I say. "But you didn't have to—"

He throws a ball that nails me right in the chest. "The jerk is right. You stink."

I'm rubbing my chest. "Maybe we should get you some anger management."

"Why would I want to manage it? Then it would be gone."

"Ya, we wouldn't want that."

"No. Now, where were we? Right, how bad you stink."

"Right. I don't actually stink."

The windup, the pitch.

"Ow, will you cut that out?"

"You cut it out. Stop wasting all Grampus's money. I'm going to need that money someday for big rings and cars and stuff when this place belongs to me."

"It's still early. Give me a chance. We don't know how good I might get. Remember, Grampus saw something in me."

"That's another thing. Grampus is insane."

"He is not insane."

"No? Have you seen him today? Earlier he was down digging up the new fifteenth hole wearing nothing but a kilt. And he says he's decided to go on until we have twenty-seven holes and an Olympic-size swimming pool."

"Ooh. Why would he want to do that?"

"Because nobody else has that, is what he says."

"Well, still. It sounds nice," I say, though it sounds scarier than nice.

"Ya, nice. And did he show you the new can't-miss invention?"

"No. How come you got to see? He didn't show anybody else. He says it's top secret."

"Well, nobody else cares like I do. If you cared enough to break into his workshop like I did, you too could have seen that the new invention is a square baseball. That's his big idea. He's going to invent a whole new pastime, make the first field right here at the complex—the playing field is shaped like Batman's bat signal, by the way—manufacture the equipment himself, then have *us* put on demonstrations for investors like a couple of half-wit monkeys chasing a square baseball.

He has elaborate plans all drawn up, right down to us in our outfits that look like basketball shirts over kilts."

"Holy smokes," I say.

"Holy smokes is right, we'll be a pair of dingle-berry pies in those outfits."

"I don't think that's the worst of it, Egon."

"No, it isn't. The worst of it is that he thinks *your* golf is going to make us all rich and famous. That's a lot crazier than a square baseball, I'll tell ya."

"Stop calling him crazy."

"Ever since he saw that movie about Howard Hughes, the world's richest maniac, it's like that's his new role model."

"He's not a maniac, Egon. He's just ambitious."

"Ambitious as a bedbug."

"Is he still down at the fifteenth?"

"No, that was early. When I left him he was still sleeping on his drafting table while I was looking at all his stuff. You know, the square baseball can be kind of unpredictable fun, bouncing it off a wall . . ."

"He was asleep the whole time?"

"The whole time. You know, I don't think he goes home at all anymore."

"We need to talk to Meredith."

She is at the desk, setting up a group of four mothers for golf. They are the mothers from Egon's kiddies' lesson. The kiddies are safely someplace else.

"Meredith," I say after they've gone, "is Grampus kind of crazy, do you think?"

"Out of his tree. Always has been." She takes a sip of her lemonade through a straw. The way she sips through a straw makes her look like a little kid. Then she lets go and her face goes instantly back to scary. It's like a hologram.

"How come I never noticed?" Egon demands.

"Because you're worse than he is," she says.

I can't let them get at each other or we'll be here all day. "Well, don't you think we should . . . do something about it?"

"No," she says bluntly. Sip, sweet face. Stop, scary face. "It doesn't bother me if he wants to be that way, I still love the old beanbag. I probably wouldn't recognize him if he gathered up his marbles again."

Just then Grampus walks through the shop in his lonesome wee kilt, passes us by wordlessly, and disappears into the bathroom.

"Well, I haven't seen that one before," Meredith says.

"Exactly," Egon says. "Maybe he was a little ringo-bingo before, but not like this."

"Now that you mention it," she says, "I suppose there has been a change. But I think it's just because he's stressed."

"Why should he be stressed?" I ask.

"Because he's working himself so hard."

"Why does he bother?"

Meredith rubs her fingers together in the *money money* gesture.

"So?" I say. "How rich does a person have to be?"

We hear raucous laughter outside and look as Teddy and Lukas come tumbling out of a big green convertible Jaguar.

"That rich," she says.

Egon is practically frothing at the mouth. "Ya," he says, "ya, that rich."

The two of them come in and make the maximum amount of noise and scene as Meredith sets them up for another day of golfing and laughing and showing off while further polluting the chunky cesspool of my brother's mind. They book eighteen holes, one cart, and one ratfink caddy.

When they are out and on their way, Meredith

continues staring at them and holding her chin. "That's his problem," she says. "Grandad wants to be a guy like that. But he's not a guy like that and he never will be, thank goodness."

"He's already rich. Isn't that good enough?"

"He's not rich, Jock. He's far from rich."

"How do you know that?"

"Listen, maybe you should go check on him. He's been in there for a while."

This is true. My grandfather has never been one of those guys to take a book into the bathroom and make a field trip out of it. He doesn't like wasting time, and once told me that anyone who enjoys spending their time in the bathroom should be chained up and made to live in there, see how they like it then.

"Grampus?" I say close to the door. I wonder if maybe he's fallen asleep again.

"Are they gone?" he asks quietly.

"Ya, they're out on the course," I tell him.

Right away the door opens and he is standing there, tall and lean and tanned. Thin and stringy and weathered. In his kilt.

"You were hiding from them?" I ask, and I want to slap myself as soon as I have said it.

"Of course not," he says, walking past me. "I'm just not appropriately dressed for greeting customers."

I follow him across the pro shop, wave at my sister on the way, and we go outside together.

"Where are you going?" he asks.

"I'm going with you, to work on the fifteenth."

"Don't be crazy. You're staying here to work on your game."

"I don't *have* a game, Grampus."

He stops and turns to face me. "What are you talking about?"

"I mean, I am no golfer. I mean, I stink."

He doesn't want to know.

"Go work on your game, Jock," he says, walking away from me. "It's just going to take some time and effort to develop, that's all. Someone like you should not be wasting his life digging holes like someone like me."

He could not have stopped me more effectively if he had wheeled around and punched me in the stomach. It feels like he did.

I stand there watching him walk, his proud, tight stride, all the muscles in his back visible and all of them flexing, and it hits me. This is not a crazy man. This is a sad man.

"What do you *mean*, someone like you?" I demand.

He just waves and keeps walking.

"I want to *be* someone like you," I say.

"Aim higher," he says.

9

THE ROOT OF ALL EVIL

"Yes, he is rich. Therefore, *we* are rich."

"Egon, your eggs are severely scrambled. We are so not rich."

He looks at his plate. His eggs are not scrambled, they are fried. But it's still early and I am afraid I have confused him.

It's a rare morning when Egon, Meredith, and I are sitting together having breakfast. She's made us bacon and eggs and toast and fried tomatoes.

"I'm not eating those," Egon says, pointing at the tomatoes as if they have just slithered under the door out of the backyard.

"So don't," Meredith says. "Who cares about your

nutrition and whether your brain ever attains its full size."

"I have attained my full brain-size already," Egon says.

She reaches across the table and pats his hand. "Oh, you poor thing."

"Meredith, will you explain to the poor thing that we are not anywhere near rich, and we never will be?"

"We are not rich, Thing, and we never will be."

"Speak for yourselves. I am going to be rich, that's for sure. Why are these tomatoes still here?"

I scoop the tomatoes off his plate. "I've decided," I say, "that the old saying is true, that money is the root of all evil."

"I thought Egon was the root of all evil?" Meredith asks seriously.

"Well obviously, first Egon, then right behind him is money."

Egon only objects to half of this statement. "Would you two stop picking on money? Money is great. Money is the most important thing there is, because it buys all the other things."

"Egon," I say, "when you look in the mirror, is there anything there?"

The doorbell rings and I am happy to leave Meredith to handle Mr. Soulless.

I'm stunned to find, when I open the door, my grandmother. She hasn't come up from Florida for maybe two years, and whenever she does visit she does it with no warning. Like now. Even if you knew she was coming, she would be a sight, standing in your doorway. She's almost six feet tall and looks like the remains of a good athlete. She was a cheerleader once, a professional coach of other cheerleaders, and she looks like she could still pull it off today. Her hair, swept straight back, manages to be both silver and gold, and she never doesn't look elegant even in a very Florida pale yellow tracksuit like the one she's wearing. She could easily be first lady of the United States, and if she was she would make all the other first ladies look like bag ladies.

"Grammus!" I say, hugging her. She hugs me right back, with twice the force. She is a great hugger, my grandmother, a warm and intense person in the flesh—possibly to make up for all the time her flesh is elsewhere.

"Jock," she says then, steering me around behind her, "I'd like you to meet Maxie. He's my boyfriend."

I wouldn't think that's a word people used after

the age of seventy, but there you go.

"Hi, Maxie," I say, shaking his hand. "Did you play with the '72 Miami Dolphins?"

"Oh, jeepers," Grammus says, "have you not learned by now not to listen to anything your lunatic grandfather says?"

Maybe the fact that Maxie is only about five foot four should have clued me in that he isn't NFL stock.

"How is the old crock doing, anyway?" Grammus says, leading me down the hall to the kitchen.

"He's doing well," I say. "He really loves running his own golf center."

"I'm glad we brought our clubs," Maxie says.

"Grammus!" Both Meredith and Egon say, popping up from the table when we walk in.

"It is so wonderful to see you," Meredith says. "I was really sorry you couldn't make it to my graduation."

Egon skips the niceties. Egon always skips niceties. "Grammus, Grampus hasn't paid us in weeks," is the first thing he thinks to say after not seeing his grandmother in two years.

"Finkage," I say low to him.

"Too badage," he says.

"Oh, that's terrible," Grammus says obligingly.

"How much does he owe you?" She is already rummaging in her purse. Oh, her ex-husband would not like this scene, not one little bit.

"That's okay, Grammus, we're fine," I say.

"We are not fine," Egon says. "You were just telling me yourself how poor we all are."

"That's not—"

"Oh, you must let me help," she says, pulling a thicket of bills the size of a *Harry Potter* book out of her bag.

"Yes," Egon says, his eyes bugging out, "we must."

"It is the least I can do," Grammus says, peeling off equal and excessive numbers of bills for each of us. "I am your grandmother for goodness' sake, and we are supposed to do this kind of thing. Also, while I am not strictly responsible for cash flow problems around here, I do have to acknowledge that your grandfather was very generous in our divorce settlement."

That catches everyone's attention. My grandfather has a lot of fine qualities, but he has never been in the same room with the word generous.

"He was?" Meredith asks.

"Well . . . maybe generous isn't the right word,

since it wasn't voluntary . . ."

"Ah," Meredith and I say together.

This is my grandmother's first visit to the complex, and Maxie's first exposure to the family at all. Despite this, the whole scene has a kind of carnival feel to it as we sweep through the gate and Maxie parks his big BMW right next to the door. As we step out of the car, we can hear Meredith's scooter coming along, and we see Grampus just coming from the field. The four of us stand there waiting for him, and as he comes closer into view, the reality—or unreality—of the big man registers.

He's in the kilt again, and out of the shirt.

"Outdoorsy type, is he?" Maxie says. He's doing a good job of staying as much in the neutral zone as he can, but really . . .

"Oh, my stars," Grammus says, giggling.

For his part, Grampus has just now gotten us in sharp focus. His face goes both alarmed-looking and hardened as he approaches. He goes straight for the ex.

"Welcome to my complex, Helen," he says formally.

"For goodness' sake would you put a shirt on, Gus," she says.

It's like he only now recognizes that he hasn't got one on. He looks almost cute as he half covers himself up and scuttles into the shop. He's back out in seconds, shirted, and standing again in his spot directly in front of Grammus.

"That's more like it," she says, laying one of those quality hugs on his leathery self.

Grammus is smiling broadly as the hug lingers a bit. Grampus is fighting, as his eyes look like they are trying to close, but he matches her squeeze for squeeze.

He will never admit that the split was not his idea.

"Gus, I want you to meet somebody," she says, grabbing his shoulders and turning him in the direction of Maxie. I am praying she doesn't use the word. "This is Maxie, my boyfriend."

I didn't have great hope, because the truth is my family are mostly unfiltered people and so their thoughts come out of their mouths exactly as they are assembled in their brains.

It's honest, and admirable, and refreshing, and it can hurt.

"Nice to meet you, Maxie," Grampus says, shaking hands.

"Gus, a pleasure. Helen has said some wonderful things about you."

"Really?" Grampus says. "Then she must have been saving them up for a long time."

Meredith parks her scooter next to the BMW, then proposes to get the visitors set up on the golf course. Grammus goes into the shop with her. Grampus stands there in the parking lot watching as Maxie goes to his car, pops open the trunk, and starts pulling out equipment.

Grampus is staring at the BMW. It is a beauty of a car. Egon has run up next to Maxie and is talking to him and helping him with the clubs, but mostly ogling every little detail of the machine and running his hands up and over every curve and detail inside the trunk and out.

Grampus is staring at the car, at the clubs—which you can tell from twenty yards are special, high-end clubs that we don't even carry here—and at Egon getting caught up in every bit of it. It's hard to tell which one of them is more impressed. But it's easy to tell which one is happier about it.

"Do you *see* these things?" Egon says, presenting one ladies' golf bag, fully stocked. "These things cost about as much as our house."

"Your house is too small," Grampus snaps. "Listen, I have to get back to work. Maxie, it was nice meeting you. Have a great game, hang around as long as you like. Maybe I'll catch up with you all later."

"That would be nice," Maxie says, but it doesn't look like the idea's going to go anywhere, since my grandfather is already ten strides in the direction of his digger, and halfway down the buttons of his shirt. He looks like he's escaping some kind of confinement, the way he tears his way out of the thing.

Egon and I caddy for Grammus and Maxie, not because they need it so much as just to hang around with them. It is fun as far as work goes, and even if she were not my grandmother, Grammus is the kind of lady we would always be happy to work for. Not unlike my parents, but very different at the same time, she is a combination of strong and controlled adult, and kind of a kid too. And while part of me feels like a traitor for saying so, Maxie is right up there with her, a good guy, just the right amount of goofy, and he treats my grandmother like he's on the verge of thanking her every minute for something.

And they can golf. If my short-term ambitions for long-term success in the world of sports were not defeated before, then they surely would be tested now.

You know that thing where a guy wants to trash-talk and he says, ah, you couldn't even beat my grandmother? Well, I couldn't beat my *own* grandmother. She'd mop the floor with me. You have to think, if you can say that, then the PGA tour might not be holding a spot open for you.

We are coming off the course at the end of eighteen holes ("You have to replay how many holes to make eighteen? My goodness your grandfather is the cheapest so-and-so . . . ," said Grammus) when the scene is interrupted by one of the odder sights I have experienced. As I look up the hill to the highest spot overlooking the course, there is Grampus, standing atop his digger, shirt off, kilt blowing in the breeze, arms folded across his chest. Everybody stops to look at him, because he is all but impossible to miss. He has made himself unmissable.

Grammus comes up alongside me as we stare up at him.

"Is he all right, Jock?"

"Sure, Grammus. He's just got a lot of work to do right now."

"For someone who's got a lot of work to do, he sure does look like a statue at the moment."

"I think he misses you," I say.

"Well, that's sweet. I miss him too, but I'm not going around with my shirt off over it."

We set the sanity bar pretty low around here.

"Oh, Grammus."

As they are wrapping up with Meredith at the desk, we hear the rumble of the digger right outside the door. Grammus and Maxie are just heading to the car, on their way to see Leonard and Peach at Fame&Fortune.

"Nice wheels," Grammus says of the digger.

This is him showing off. "It's mine, you know," Grampus says, still in the driver's seat. "It's not rented or anything. It's mine. I'm doing all my own work here, making improvements to the course."

"That's really great, Gus," she says. "Really great. I'm happy that you have all this for yourself, really I am. Well, we're off to see Leonard and Peach."

She heads for the big BMW, and Grampus suddenly gets a look of mild panic as he watches her go to the car.

"What about dinner?" Grampus says.

"What about it?" she calls back.

"Well, I was thinking, maybe we could all, all of us go out to dinner together someplace nice? Since you're here and all. What do you think?"

My grandmother leans into the car to see what her . . . gentleman friend thinks. She pops her head back up and says, "Great. Call us at Leonard's later."

"Great," Grampus says, and looks energized. He grinds his digger into gear and starts the slow slog back up his hill, across his golf course, back to his own work on his own land in his own digger.

It has the feel of a celebration. I don't know when the last time was I was in a real restaurant. Meredith goes sometimes, with Carlo, which is where she is tonight. But Egon and me, and our keepers, uh-uh. We are not actually restaurant people, and it shows. Leonard and Peach are about as excited as we are, and being Leonard and Peach, they are not shy about letting it be known.

"Can I order whatever I want, Dad?" Leonard asks his father.

"Of course you can," Grampus says grandly. "This is a celebration."

"Celebrations should happen every day," Peach says.

"Then they wouldn't be special," I say.

"Of course they would," Peach says. "Every day already is special. If we had a celebration every day, then people would notice that."

That's my mom. But it's beautiful nonsense thinking like that that lets her refer to Egon as "unconventionally sweet."

Grampus shakes his head. He leans over to his date, Melanie, and sort of apologizes. "I'm sorry," he says to his current golf cart lady, who happens to be younger and more sparkly than all the others, "they're like this. They're from that generation."

"I think it's lovely," Melanie says. "I am too."

Grampus looks a little embarrassed as I see Grammus do the *shame-shame* gesture at him, rubbing her index fingers together.

Egon has had four Cokes before anyone has ordered any food. My father points out he is putting poison into his body, but as usual leaves it to him to use his better judgment. Egon uses his better judgment to order himself two more Cokes.

Grampus orders champagne for all the adults. All the adults approve.

When it comes time to order food, my parents, despite their giddiness, remain true to their convictions.

"I will have the vegetarian nut loaf in spring onion gravy," Peach says, clapping her hands as if she's just been allowed to have a fudge cake main dish.

"And I will have the seafood platter," Leonard says, "but only the items with no central nervous system."

The waiter stares at my dad. My dad gives him his angelic dolphin smile. Angelic dolphin smile doesn't explain much, so the waiter looks to the boss.

"Just leave out the squid and the monkfish," Grampus says.

Grampus and his girlfriend go for the lobsters, as does Grampus's former girlfriend. Former girlfriend's boyfriend opts for filet mignon, "bloody."

"Sounds good," says Egon. "Give me two of those."

"He means burgers," Grampus says.

I have roast stuffed chicken, and I have to say as simple as it sounds it is glorious. It's a top-notch restaurant, I can tell from the prices.

Everybody loves their food. The talk is nonstop as conversation zigs and zags across the table. Leonard clicks with his father's date because they have so much in common, being exactly the same age and dealing with Grampus. Peach seems to be sweeping Maxie off his feet to the point where you might think Grammus has something to worry about, but the only immediate thing she probably needs to worry about is the grinning senior citizen in the plastic lobster bib sitting across from her.

Egon, who has had about fifteen Cokes, is calling all the adults dingleberries and the adults, who have had maybe as much champagne, are loving it. They think he's a scamp, rather than the devil.

He nudges me and directs my attention under the table. I casually drop a chicken bone and look under as I'm picking it up.

Grampus has his shoes off. He has no socks on. And he is working hard at footsying my grandmother's feet across the table. For her part, Grammus is ducking and juking all over trying to avoid him. From just the feet you would think they were dancing together.

I come back up to find Egon has lifted the remaining half of the chicken from my plate and is giving it the full Henry VIII treatment.

"You are a hog, with no conscience," I say.

"And you are a chump, with no chicken," he replies with a mouth full of my chicken.

"So, Maxie," Grampus says, filling Maxie's glass and obviously enjoying playing the host whether he actually is or not, "have you always been down in Florida?"

"Yes," Maxie says. "Lived there all my life. I think I'm the only one. And you, Gus?"

"Oh yes, this is my home."

"But not his original home," Grammus says.

The smile, so tentative and unusual on my grandfather's face, slides away now. "Yes it is."

"Oh come on now, Gus, don't be shy. I think it's a marvelous story, the way you've built your way up from—"

"No, it's not," he says.

The table has gone quieter as they face each other over the dessert menus and Grampus's past.

"Yes, it is," she says. "Gus was raised in an orphanage, in Newfoundland. Back in the days when being in an orphanage in Newfoundland was about equivalent to living on a prison ship nobody knew about."

Maxie, Egon, Melanie, and myself are surprised. Leonard, in a smooth diversion, starts reading the dessert menu out loud to Peach.

"Oh look, hon, peach cobbler . . ."

Maxie reaches across to shake Gus's hand. Gus takes it, but with no great enthusiasm.

"I'm always honored to meet a self-made man," Maxie says warmly. "Especially made against the tallest odds."

Melanie squeezes Grampus's arm with both hands.

Grampus still has on his plastic lobster bib, which comes frighteningly close to making him look cute. He must sense this because he suddenly starts clawing at the knot to get it off. He looks a little desperate when it's not coming, until Melanie gets it for him.

Egon starts nudging me to look under the table. My plate has been cleared, so I have nothing to lose this time.

Grammus is giving him some footsie. Grampus is motionless.

I come back up to find my drink all gone.

"You should drink more Coke, Egon, it really enhances your personality."

"I was noticing that myself."

Grampus, who right now seems to me to have more reason than ever to be proud of himself, looks like he's just going to slither under the table. The waiter comes to take dessert and coffee orders.

"Is the coffee fair trade?" Leonard asks.

"Of course it's fair trade," Grampus cuts in.

"How do you know that?" Leonard presses, possibly unwisely.

"Because there is a price next to it. You give them

money and they give you coffee, and that is fair trade. He'll have a coffee, waiter."

"No, thank you," Leonard says.

"Cripes, will you just have the coffee and not be a freak, for once?"

"For goodness' sake, Gus," Grammus says, "he doesn't have to have the coffee if he doesn't want it."

My father's parents are arguing over what he can order in a restaurant.

"Is this the best dinner ever, or what?"

No prizes for guessing who said that. But he's not as bad as he sounds.

"Just get the coffee," Grampus continues. "Just to pretend you can be normal for even a short while. Just to pretend, for your father, that he did something right in his miserable little life, and he raised a son who can be normal on special occasions."

My grandfather's miserable little life. How can he think that? How can he see his life and see something so different from what I think is there? It's scary is what it is, like his own existence has been a movie but he himself has had his eyes closed through the whole thing. In fact now that I think about it, his life could *be* a movie. I'd go and see it, even if he wouldn't.

"I could check and see if it is fair trade," says the

embarrassed waiter.

"No, that won't be necessary," my father says, "I'll have the coffee." Then he looks to Grampus again. "Is it okay if I have decaf?"

Grampus is just staring at the table now. The waiter makes the rounds and everyone orders. Considering it is dessert, it is a pretty somber affair.

"On and on it goes, eh, Gus?" Grammus says. "You still haven't figured out how it all works."

"I have figured out how it all works," he answers quietly. "That's what's wrong."

With that, Melanie takes her napkin from her lap, wipes the corners of her mouth politely, and drops the napkin on her plate. "I think I've had enough," she says, and pushes away from the table.

"Oh, no," Grammus says, "please don't go."

Grampus remains slumped and silent.

"Thank you," Melanie says. "It was nice meeting you all. I'll just get a cab."

She is gone.

"Can I have her dessert?"

He is not as bad as he sounds.

"I think we're about done, too," Grammus says, and she and Maxie place their napkins on their plates. Leonard and Peach follow.

"Waiter," Maxie says, "Check, please."

"No, no," Grampus says.

"Oh, no," Grammus agrees, but in a different way. "Gus has to do this."

"Oh, he does not have to do this. I'd really like—"

"Oh, but he does," Grammus says. She leans way over the table toward him. "You do, don't you? You *have* to do this, don't you, Gus?"

It is some kind of challenge. Some kind of test from her to him. I have no idea what he wins if he passes the test, but it does seem somehow important. He pauses a long time as he struggles with his answer, as a film of sweat glistens on his cheeks.

"I do have to do it," he blurts as the waiter arrives and Grampus shoves his credit card at him.

Grammus shakes her head sadly. It is obvious for all to see that the old man is taking no pleasure out of his treating everybody to an expensive dinner. In fact, it seems to be causing him immense stress. I don't know very much about Maxie, but the signs are that he could pay for all this with the change that you could find in the big plush seats of his car.

But my grandfather just *has* to.

"I was hoping to find you different, Gussie,"

Grammus says, reaching a hand across the table to him. She is being very soft with him, like he could break.

"I am different," he says unconvincingly.

"Yes," she says, "you're worse. You still don't realize what you've got. You have finally once and for all hardened into one of those pathetic people who know the price of everything and the value of nothing."

Egon leans close to me and says, "I don't get it. Is there a difference?"

Grampus looks dazed, tired, and battered like a boxer who is taking punishment without the luxury of being able to fall down. He looks over to Maxie and says, "I didn't get to show you my snooker table, did I? It's one-of-a-kind. Priceless. Would you like to come by tomorrow and see it?"

Like his *things* are all he has. To prove that he *is*.

"We'll be gone," Grammus says.

The waiter comes back and is looking grim. He bends low and says to Grampus quietly, but not quietly enough, "I'm sorry, sir, but your credit card has been refused."

There is a scramble as Leonard and Peach go into their pockets and Grammus whips out her purse, but Maxie appears to be a veteran of getting the check quickly, and he's on it. The waiter and Maxie disappear together to sort things out.

Meanwhile my grandfather does not so much as twitch. He sits there with his feeble card in his feeble hand and he looks all of his age plus mine, and yours, and everybody's at the table.

Egon has nothing to say. I look over to find him looking like he never, ever looks. Concerned. He looks unsettled. He cannot stop staring at Grampus.

"You should call your bank first thing," my dad says to his dad. "I'm sure there is something fishy. That identity theft business is everywhere now, and I'll bet that's what happened to you. Get that sorted right out, Dad, so they don't get everything."

"Yes," Grampus says. "I'm sure that's what it is. I'll get it sorted right out. Thank you, son."

Maxie comes back and everybody thanks him as modestly as possible for buying us all this sensational dinner.

Even Egon is tactful, in his way, silently smacking Maxie on the behind like a baseball player.

When we file out of the restaurant, it's just like a funeral.

10

THE VALUE OF EVERYTHING

Grampus has given everybody the day off.

I don't like it.

Not only do I go in, but I go in extra early because I can't sleep. As I park my bike, I can already hear the sound of his digger over the hill.

By the time I get down there, I notice the machine is not moving. It's just plunked there, in a hole of its own making, the engine *grrr*ing away, but nothing actually going on. I go right up to it, and there's the owner, driver, master of his universe.

He's not moving. I call to him and I get nothing. I jump up on the side of the digger and lean into the little cab.

He is wearing the clothes from the restaurant the night before. He has been here since he left the restaurant, and now he is here motionless. His eyes are half closed, his hands at his sides, his head tilted, and his facial features all wrong like they are melting right off his face.

I turn off the engine and bomb to the office to call an ambulance.

A minor stroke. That's what they say he's had, but I find the concept a little hard to grasp. How can something like a stroke be minor? How can something happen inside your head that changes the way you sound, the way you move, the way you look, even, and it's minor? How can a person's whole world be changed by something that's considered in any way minor?

Because it could be a lot worse, is why. My grandfather can talk, he can eat, he can think pretty clearly, and he can walk. He just can't do any of that as well as he could before.

And he is different. In another way.

I have heard of this condition where a person goes into a coma, and when they wake up they are speaking in some foreign accent. I heard it on the radio. This one lady was knocked out with an English accent and woke up speaking like she was from Jamaica. And this Canadian guy went out sounding like any other frozen farm boy, then got bopped on the head by a hay bale and came out of it sounding like something out of a Russian spy movie.

That has not happened to my grandfather. But he's changed.

"Who on this earth needs his own digging machine?" Grampus says in his slow, deliberate slur. We have all been taking turns visiting him, and right now it's me and Egon sitting watch and encouraging him to eat his lunch.

"You?" I ask.

He shakes his head. "What is a guy way past retirement doing digging up a golf course with a machine that costs more than your house when there are plenty of companies who would do the job for a fraction of the cost?"

"And do it a lot better," Egon points out helpfully.

"Yes," Grampus admits.

"Can I have your juice?" Egon asks.

"No," Grampus says.

"Can I have your apple?"

"No," I snap.

"Can I have the digger, then?"

"Egon!" I shout.

"What? He said he doesn't want it anymore. I'm just trying to make him happy. Is it *so* wrong for a guy to try and make his dying grandfather happy?"

You probably think you know how sickening Egon's little play looks up close. You have no idea.

"He's not dying, you animal."

Grampus's roommate is in something like a coma, since he never seems to wake up for more than five seconds at a time. Still, he must be thrilled not to get visitors like us.

Grampus, however, is laughing, in his spooky, stretched out, slo-mo strokey way. I don't even know if I have ever seen him actually laughing out loud, but that is exactly what he is doing.

"Ah, boys," he says, "you are a tonic for the old man, I have to tell you."

Egon looks stunned. "See, I told you he's dying."

"And I told you you're an animal."

"I am not dying. And yes, he is an animal."

"Grampus!" Egon is clearly both mortified and flattered.

"But it's okay," Grampus says, "there is still time for you. You can change."

"I can, but I won't."

"Sure you will," Grampus says.

"No," I say, "he's right, he won't."

"I have faith," Grampus says. "You can be wrong-headed and foolish for a long time, and still come out of it if you get the right jolt. Like I got. Like you're going to get."

"I'm going to get a jolt?" Egon asks warily.

Grampus nods excitedly. As excitedly, anyway, as a bed-bound old dude can.

"Yessss," I say, pumping my fist. "Egon's finally getting electric shock therapy."

"Is that it?" Egon asks.

"No, not that I know of. No, I'm talking about lifestyle changes. I am lifting some of our needless burdens."

"Such as?" Egon is deeply suspicious now. Which is good.

"I've removed you from my will."

When I say Egon throws himself on the floor here, I mean, Egon *throws* himself right down on the white tile floor. The roommate opens his eyes then squeezes them tight again. I think he might be faking.

"Just because *you* have a stroke, Grampus, why do *I* have to lose all the *stuff*?"

Grampus limply waves Egon up off the floor and close to him. Egon obeys, probably hoping there is still something to be gained.

"Because *stuff* will kill you, my boy. And because I love you."

Now I very nearly hit the floor. I heard my grandfather use the L-word about a person only once before, and that was when the president announced tax cuts for small businesses.

What do you say? For this moment, everybody in the room has had a stroke.

Grampus takes advantage of the situation to drive it all home.

"My digger, my golf carts, my complex, it's all been *stuff*. It's no different from that godawful ring you took from Teddy that you thought I didn't know about."

I hear a loud gulp. It's me.

"You're a spooky old man now," is Egon's version of a gulp.

"Yes, and having that ring, having that gaudy terrible secret, it has been a bit of a curse for you, hasn't it?"

Well, even the new Grampus can't get everything right.

"No," Egon says effortlessly. "The curse has been not being able to wear it, but now that's over with."

"It's not a sign of strength. It's weakness. It doesn't make you happy. It doesn't, I swear to you. I can see by your face, Egon, that you don't believe me, but you will. Someday you will. Meantime, I'm not making you any worse by heaping meaningless possessions on you. I'm leaving the complex to your parents."

Egon reacts.

"Would you get up off the floor?" Grampus says.

Having nothing obvious still to gain, Egon refuses. He lies motionless on the floor.

Grampus turns to me. "You know what's my idea of a great day? You know what's been great about my life at the complex, Jock?"

"I'm guessing it's not all the *stuff*."

"You're guessing correctly. The greatest thing is going an entire workday with no shoes on."

He does love cool feet. I look down at them now and, sure enough, he's got one foot poking out of the blankets on either side, hanging over the edges of the bed. Even for feet they are pretty famously grotesque feet, the baby toes looking like flesh-colored balls, meat-grapes dangling there out to the sides.

"And no shirt," I remind him.

"And my kilt," he says. "You can bet the marines and the city never let me wear that on the job."

Egon feels the need to reengage. He stays flat on the floor, though.

"Leonard and Peach are going to totally freak out the complex."

"Let 'em," Grampus says.

"It'll be completely weird. You should see what they're doing already. Even the food. They won't serve anything with a central nervous system."

"That's okay with me," Grampus says, "I barely have one myself now."

Ever the optimist, Egon is convinced that once Grampus sees the way my parents have been running the place in his absence, he'll go on a rampage and put everything back where it belongs—such as us, in the will.

The day Leonard picks his father up from the hospital, Egon has his busiest day of the whole year. He's going around the pro shop lighting incense and making sure the new age space music is playing on the stereo. He takes Peach's stand-up sign advertising her palm reading and manicuring from Fame&Fortune and sets it up just outside the front door.

"You see," Peach says to Meredith, giving her boy a big squeeze, "didn't I tell you there was a good boy inside here?" She shakes him. "There is a good boy inside here."

Meredith can only laugh. "Did Egon eat him?"

We are all standing like a hotel staff waiting for inspection when my dad and his dad come through the door. Grampus is using a cane on one side and his son on the other and while it's all pretty slow, it's not as bad as I expected.

Peach goes straight up and hugs Grampus, and he looks like he's about to fall. But there is no chance of that as she holds on to him like a human body cast.

"Now listen," she says, leading him around. "You are going to see a lot of changes, but I just felt they could not be avoided. As soon as I walked in here that first day when we started, I could feel that the energy was all wrong in here. All wrong. The space was wrong, the flow was wrong. And all that meat and microwaving certainly didn't help things. It was a big cosmic mess, which, I think, was part of your trouble, Gus. Am I right, Leonard?"

"She's right there, Dad. The shui was completely fenged up in here."

Grampus nods at everything, smiling in a newly

grandfatherly way. He picks up a menu off one of the rearranged tables in the sparkling clean café.

"Hummus?" he says out loud. "Baba ghanoush?"

Peach is beaming.

Grampus sits down, tired already, but that's okay for now. "How is business?" he asks.

"Business is good," she says. "Word is spreading, and we are getting all different kinds of people coming in."

Leonard announces grandly, "We have thrown open the gates to the citadel of privilege, making it a welcoming place for the common man and falafel."

Meredith translates. "He means we're getting a lot more non-golf types now."

"Freaks," Grampus says.

"Yup," Meredith says.

"Enough to pay the bills?"

"Not really."

"Well, once I sell the digger and a lot of the other nonsense, we'll get the ship right."

Peach has knelt down and is gently slipping Grampus's shoes off. He lets out a sigh of pure joy. He closes his eyes.

"Rats," Egon says, "he likes it. He likes it. His brain has been permanently damaged, and so everything's ruined. We have to do something."

"What could we possibly do?"

"I'll tell you what we can do. *Something*. That's what we can do."

It may sound like my brother hasn't really got any big ideas, but that's the problem. The smaller his ideas, the bigger his actions.

11

TEMPORARY INSANITY

There are important things here, beautiful things and sad things jamming right up into each other in every corner of the complex, in every corner of every day now. Our long hot summer of being nothing but lucky and tanned and kings of the world has melted into something altogether different.

The complex is truly complex now, not the simple sports-and-money field it was when summer started.

Not that you'd know it from listening to Egon.

"It'll pass," he says, busying himself with the controls of Grampus's digger.

"What do you mean, 'It'll pass'? The man has had a *stroke*, Egon, not a cough. It's not gonna pass. He is who he is now, and *you* have to get over it more than he does."

He's staring at the controls of the digger, pulling levers, kicking at something.

"How do I make it go?"

"You don't make it go," I say. "You get out of there."

"The only way I'm leaving is driving away in this. Those guys are going to be here in an hour, and I have to save this machine from them. I have to save Grampus from himself. He just needs time, and in the meantime while he's getting his marbles back, I have to make sure nothing crazy happens."

"So you're stealing your grandfather's digger."

"Correct."

"So that nothing *crazy* happens."

"Go away," Egon says, and emphasizes by starting up the machine. *Gruum*, it says, and before you know it, Egon's yanking levers back and forth, whooping like a screech monkey, and jerking the poor honest machine side-to-side and left-right like it's having convulsions. It doesn't take him long (they are both simple machines) before he's got it responding, and I am being pursued.

"Egon!" I shout, running backward from him.

"This isn't funny."

His expression is puzzled. "What are you talking about? Of course it is."

It was stupid to try and reason with him even that much, so I turn and bolt.

He's laughing so hard behind me, it's louder than the digger's motor. He's laughing not in that exaggerated, I'm-gonna-get-you way, but in a really happy, helpless cackle like he's just heard the best joke of his life. He's right at my back, and it's getting hairy serious, and I have no doubt at all that he'll knock me down, when suddenly he pulls back.

I'm gasping as I finally can slow down and turn. He has stopped, and is frantically working the thing around in spasms to get it going in the other direction. He's clearly in a panic over something, and I turn the other way to see.

The cavalry is arriving to rescue me. My grandfather, driving one golf cart, and Teddy and Lukas driving in the other, steaming our way, uphill, at a brisk four miles per hour.

"You can't have it," Egon shouts as the stress of the situation overcomes him. He is now spinning the digger in a circle, not quite as fast as the teacup ride at the carnival, but close enough for laughs. Teddy and Lukas and Grampus have now reached the scene and parked. Like the cops reaching the scene after chasing the dangerous criminal a long way, the two men pile out of their cart and swagger toward the digger.

Grampus does not swagger, of course. My grandfather's swagger has gone. He sits in the driver's seat of his golf cart, one of his fleet of two golf carts. Which will, when this is over, be a fleet of one. He sits in his cart, which is what he does throughout the day most days now. He's like a decrepit little film director motoring around the set, only without the power and the glamour. I imagine this is what he will do for most of his days from here on, as he sits and he watches.

I watch him watch as another big piece of his small empire is dislodged. He takes it in silence.

Egon does no such thing. He is loud and he is foul and he is not giving an inch. Nobody can coax him out of the digger, not with food or flattery or threats. Not even with money. In the end measures get drastic and since Egon knows no such creature as compromise, the day peaks with Egon in the digger, the digger (along with one golf cart and one formerly priceless snooker table) on the back of a flatbed, and the flatbed rumbling off down the gravel drive.

"Don't be a jerk," I call to him.

"I'm standing up for what's right," he says, all perversely heroic about it.

"It's only stuff," I say.

Now he becomes a kind of greedy philosopher. "Everything is stuff. Stuff is everything."

"We don't need all the stuff," I say.

"Where the stuff goes, I go," he says.

I have cared about as much as I can now. I start waving good-bye. "Fine," I say, "that gets rid of useless machinery *and* reduces payroll. Have a nice life."

"I will. Try not to miss me."

It doesn't even require a response.

Teddy reassures us that he will return the boy when he comes to his senses. I tell him in that case we won't be expecting him for dinner.

"It's my fault," Grampus says, sitting sadly at the little wheel of his little cart. He's got watery eyes and a bumpy sound in his voice as he watches his stuff and his old friend and his grandson fade away. "I poisoned the boy with the money-love."

I hop over into the passenger seat next to him. "It is not your fault, Grampus. Trust me, he was poisoned way before you got to him."

It's a long, awkward, quiet couple of minutes as we sit there in the cart in the empty lot, and somehow I don't think he's convinced.

12

THE MONEY SHOT

Things have been slow, and the truth is that we have only seen pay coming our way once or twice the whole summer. So Meredith started telling me to come in later or sometimes not at all. I still come in pretty much every day, but I stagger my hours, staying home until the afternoon sometimes. Meredith is taking over the day-to-day running of things more and more, making the decisions from her command post at the front desk, while Grampus tools around in his golf cart like a mute, motorized ghost.

"Your doppelgangers are here," she says as I walk in one morning.

"My what?"

"Your doppelgangers. You know, those two guys who are exactly like you and Egon?"

"The Nobletts? Meredith, are you referring to the Nobletts? You think they are like us? They are nothing like us. I can't think of any two guys who are less like us than the Nobletts are. That's ridiculous."

"Right. Well, they are here."

"Call Egon," I say desperately. "Get him down here right away."

"What am I, your secretary?"

"Hey, you're responsible. You're the one who released the hellhounds into our peaceful kingdom."

"Dramatic much, Jock? Anyway, what do you expect me to do, turn away paying customers because you're afraid of them?"

"I am not afraid of them. And yes, turn them away. I would pay you just as much to keep them out. What did they pay for, anyway, a bucket o' balls?" Oh, please, let it be a bucket o' balls. Please let them just be here for a half hour or so on the driving range.

"Day passes."

The dreaded day passes. That means they have paid the flat fee that gives them access to all areas of my life for the full, entire day of doing whatever tickles their moronic fancies.

"Day passes, huh?"

"Yup."

"Maybe they'll get bored. Most people don't stay all day even if they have day passes. I'm sure we don't have enough here to keep them—"

"All day. They aren't going anywhere. They've already ordered their lunches. And the way their parents unloaded them in the parking lot—like the mafia dumping bodies off the highway—and tore screaming away, I don't think they will be expected to leave here one minute early."

"See, *everybody* hates them."

"Well, they don't seem to feel that way about you. They asked me to let them know when you arrive."

"Aw, crap. Come on, get Egon on the phone, hurry."

She puts the phone up on the counter instead. "Do your own dirty work, Braveheart."

"I will," I say, then I dial and wait.

"House of Egon," answers the voice on the other end.

"Would you stop answering the phone that way?"

"Casa Egon."

"It is not your house."

"Planet Egon—you're just living on it."

"They're here, Egon."

"They are, are they?"

"Yes."

"Do they want to take you with them, or will it be just a quick probe and back to their spaceship?"

"Well, they're not aliens, but you're not far off. It's the nemeses."

Not such a snap answer this time.

"The Nobletts? Are there, at *our* complex?"

"Yup."

I expect to hear him burst out the door, his tires screeching down the driveway before he even hangs up. I have it quite wrong.

"I guess you're in deep sneakers, then," he says, and I can hear his oily smile right through the phone.

"You are kidding. Are you trying to tell me you're not coming right down for this?"

"I'm really sorry, but Meredith says I'm not on the payroll anymore."

"Egon . . ."

"This is just business, Jock. You know I have a very expensive lifestyle. And you seem to have moved your secret money hiding spot, so that's going to take me even more time looking this morning. Are you scared enough to pay me yourself?"

"I am not scared," I say a little too loudly. Meredith splutters a laugh.

"That's the spirit, little man," he says, and hangs up.

I stare at the phone for a minute. The first twenty seconds are rage, the middle twenty jittery indecision, and the final twenty resolution. There would be nothing more degrading than calling him back, and I know, know, *know*, he is staring at the phone on his end as well. It's like we can have a standoff without even being in the same place, without even having a linkup.

"Where are they, Meredith?" I ask wearily.

"Out on the course. They are playing the front nine before lunch. But you can't meet them, anyway, because your pro is here."

"My *what* is here?"

"Your pro. Mastodon Monty. Rufus the Goofus."

"Why is he here again? I thought we had settled this already? I stink. I don't want to play, and he doesn't want to teach me."

"Yes, well, this is generally agreed. But since Grampus had to pay him for three lessons up front, and because that's probably three more lessons than our alleged *pro* has been paid for all year . . . he's waiting for you at the driving range."

"Is he even a real pro?"

"I couldn't tell you. But he doesn't even have his own clubs. He borrows a set whenever he comes here."

"Sheesh," I say, grabbing *my* driver out of *my* bag and feeling pretty stupid that I can even say that.

"So, we meet again," he says as I approach him at bay eight of the range. He doesn't even look up—that is rule number one after all—as he speaks. He whacks a drive that goes pretty straight and pretty far for a guy who doesn't own his own clubs.

"That's a great drive," I say.

"Thanks," he says. "Now, if I could only do that consistently, *and* add about fifty percent in length, I'd still have my PGA tour card."

"You don't have one? Isn't that what your fliers in the pro shop advertise? That you're a PGA tour pro?"

Now he looks at me. "What? Of course I have a PGA tour card. What are you talking about? How do you think I met Davis Love the third? Think I met him at the supermarket or something? You think Davis Love the third just bumps around the supermarkets all day and that's where I met him?"

"It's possible."

"Well, I didn't. I met him on the tour. Now come here and let's work on your grip."

If you ask me, I'd say Don Monty's grip needs a lot more work than mine does. His grip on reality, I mean, which appears to be very loose. But since nobody asked me and nobody is likely to, I have to volunteer the information.

"Time's up," I say.

"Excuse me?"

"Time's up. The lesson's over."

"I've only been here ten minutes."

"Right. Bye. And the next lesson's over too, so no need to come back."

"Sure," he says. "Fine. Whatever." He walks right past me, huffing, stripping off his glove. Just as he's by me I reach out and snag the driver out of his hand. I somehow don't feel confident he'll make his way all the way to the clubhouse to return it.

"I'll take care of this for you," I say. "And my grandfather is going to be anxious to see that tour card of yours, if you're planning to hang around his club anymore. I'm anxious to see it too. This'll be exciting."

He throws his hands up *so what* style and keeps walking.

"Your loon of a grandfather would be anxious to see any cards he could. He's not playing with a full deck himself."

"You shut up," I shout. "You don't know what you're talking about. And you're a fake. So don't bother coming back here even if you have a card, because it's not welcome at this club."

"If there's even going to *be* a club before long."

"What's that supposed to mean?"

"Work on your grip, kid," he calls, and is gone.

And that is the end of our relationship. The end of my formal learning experience in golf. What have I learned? Well, it seems once again that there may be truth in the notion that much of life is contained in the small world of this one ancient and honorable sport. Because I might never have learned of the existence of the likes of Don Monty if I had not met him here. I might not have believed he could have existed if I had not met him in the flesh.

Perhaps it is a knowledge I could have lived without.

Perhaps I will work on my grip.

My grandfather is a fine guy, and Don Monty is not. There's nothing wrong with my grandfather's mind, except maybe people like Don Monty. And if that's what makes you crazy, then maybe crazy is better.

There is a near-full bucket o' balls at my feet, and I have two drivers and the sudden feeling that I can do this. Based on nothing other than the absolute wrongness of the man who told me how bad I was, I am filled with confidence. I take that confidence out on the bucket o' balls.

What did he mean if there's even going to be a club? What a creep. Of course there will be a club. There will always be a club.

I need to hit some drives.

Holy smokes it feels good.

"You stink."

I do not know for how long I have had a gallery watching. But it is a gallery of two.

Concentration is key. Don't let the rabble rattle you. I keep my feet planted, my head down. I hold my form, I maintain my grip. This is golf, this is life.

And I splay balls all over the place in the most ridiculous fashion. The Nobletts are laughing so hard from their spot along the fence to my left, it causes an echo effect inside the driving bays and makes it sound like I am being mocked by a whole village of one-note barbarian nosepicker people like themselves. It gets worse when one spectacularly mis-hit ball actually ricochets back up over my head, crashes into the bay structure above and behind me, and clangs around the steel-and-tin frame like a bullet in a Yosemite Sam cartoon.

The Nobletts sound like they will die with laughter, but I don't have that kind of luck. I take a small—invisible to human perception, that kind of small—moral victory in finishing my bucket o' balls before beginning the long slink back to the clubhouse dragging my two drivers behind me.

As I exit the wooden door that leads out of the bays and onto the paved path, I realize I won't be slinking anyplace just yet.

"Those are some nice drivers," Herb says as the Nobletts come way up close to me.

"Yes, they are," I say, attempting to go around them.

"Can we try 'em?" Albie asks.

"You have a whole bag of clubs right there," I say, pointing out the pointless.

"Ya, but you're some kind of pro. You have a coach and your own golf course and everything, so your equipment must be way great. Can we try?"

"It's not really my golf course."

Herb grabs one of the drivers out of my hand. I

grab it back. I'm trying to hold on to the two clubs tightly, but it's awkward and I wind up losing both of them. Now each of the Noblett brothers is holding one of the drivers, standing next to their bag of perfectly good clubs, and I am standing, clubless, with my back against the enclosure wall.

They size up the clubs, checking their heads, checking for weight and balance, taking mini-swings. The one Albie has, belonging to the complex, is a Slazenger Red Hot Extreme. The other one, mine, is a Slazenger Fastrax 400 Anti-Slice. They are good clubs, somewhere short of top-of-the-line but certainly more club than I'll ever need, more club than anyone I know will ever need.

"I think I need this club," Herb says, sticking mine in his bag. Albie hands me back the Red Hot.

"You don't need it. You need to give it back to me. My grandfather gave that to me."

Not only do I know how useless that statement is, how titanically ol' Herb is going to *not* care about my sentimental attachment to this piece of sporting equipment, but I also know how counterproductive it is because it hands him a whopping fat opportunity for ridicule and viciousness. Problem is, like about half of what I say under pressure, I only know these things after the words are out of me.

First the two of them laugh for about a minute and a half. Then Herb gets the strength and gets to the point. "You rich people make me want to puke. Just have grampy pampy buy you a hundred new clubs and stop whining. While he's at it he can get me a new bike to replace the one your idiot brother lost in the lake."

"The bike has nothing to do with me. And hold on. You think I'm *rich*?"

The very topic, the very word, makes the eyes in Herb's head roll backward as he spits it. "*Rich*? You are *rich*. Everybody knows you're *rich*." He looks like a psychotic blinking pinball machine.

"That's a joke," I spit back.

"You see me laughin'?"

"No. No, Herb, I don't believe I do. But that doesn't matter. Give me the club back."

Albie, being older and presumably more mature than Herb since a whoopee cushion is more mature than Herb, seems to be losing some interest.

"You really need the club, Herb?"

The psychotic pinball machine turns on its brother. "Yes. I really need the club."

"He really needs the club," Albie says with a shrug.

"He can't have it," I say.

"Give him one of your other clubs, for a trade," Albie says to Herb.

"I need all my clubs."

Albie shrugs again. He might be less evil than Herb, but he's not a lot more articulate.

"I know," Herb says, "I'll play ya for it."

Ah, cripes. I was getting used to the idea I was going to have to fight him for it. This is unbearable.

"No," I say calmly.

Herb looks flustered. "You can't say no. I have your club. You need to play me for it. You're the big rich-boy pro golfer, and I have your club that your stupid senile old grandfather gave you, so you have to play me."

There are so many things in there that he's saying that I want to jump all over. Except for the fact that he is such a tense bulb-eyed freak and this is so clearly making him furious, so I don't really have to do much at all to get to him.

"Nope," I say chirpily.

"Then I'm keeping your club."

"No, you're not."

"Then I'm giving you a beating."

"*You* stole *my* club, and you have to give *me* a beating for it."

Albie has now progressed to embarrassed. "Make *sense*, Herb," he says, flustered.

To nobody's surprise, Herb declines to make sense.

"Are you going to play me in golf, or am I going to have to beat you with your own club?"

"I'm going to talk to that chick at the front desk," Albie says.

"That *chick* is my sister," I say defiantly. I have no idea what I had hoped to achieve there.

"Okay," Albie says, and heads to the shop.

Then there are two. It almost strikes me as funny, being in this absurd situation, with this absurd science project of a person. I almost wish there was another conscious, thinking being here to share the silliness with.

But when I turn back to consider the possibilities and consider my nemesis, I see his face. His eyes and behind them.

This is rage. This is scary rage and hatred and too true violence I am standing with here. Herb Noblett hates me, intensely, and though it makes no sense to me at all, it doesn't make the situation any less real. His eyes are all but bleeding, they are so liquid and red. His teeth are bared and grinding and his chest is rising and falling, his nostrils wide open. A race horse on drugs probably looks a lot like this.

"Would you calm down?" I say.

He chooses not to.

Without warning, Herb lunges at me. He grabs me by the neck, and before I know it I am spun, flipped, and on my back. Herb is sitting on my chest and has my arms pinned by his knees. I want to tell him how stupid this is, and as I open my mouth to do just that, he fills it with his fist. I take the money shot, right in the mouth, and right away I taste my own blood running over my teeth and tongue to the back of my throat.

And as quick as all that happens, he's even quicker jumping up off me and bolting away, toward the open spaces of the course and beyond, the bag of clubs clattering on his back.

I'm lying here, stunned, staring at a sky that is getting threatening with fat dark clouds. Then the clouds themselves are blocked out as Albie's head floats into my view, upside down. He's eating a Tootsie Pop.

"Your sister gave me this," he says, waving the pop at me. "To go away. I like her." If Albie notices anything amiss here, it is not apparent. "Where's Herb?"

I point in the direction of the golf course.

"Thanks," he says. As he steps over me he points at my mouth with his Tootsie Pop. "You shouldn't have antagonized him. He has a real problem with rich people."

"*What* rich people?" I splutter.

I don't get even a short break before that head is replaced by another, and the clouds just don't have a chance. It's my grandfather's head. My lameness has inspired a rare trip out of his golf cart, and he is teetering over me with the help of his aluminum cane.

"Did that first hoodlum leave with one of your clubs?" he asks me.

"You were watching," I say.

"Sorrily, I was," he says sorrily.

"I suppose he does have a club belonging to me," I say.

"I suppose that situation will be rectified," he says.

"I suppose it will."

Grampus takes a deep, deep breath. He leans back and looks up at the heavy-to-bursting dark clouds as he speaks. "You know, you are going to meet a lot of bullies of one kind or another in this world, Jock. More bullies than gents, that's for sure. And learning to deal with them is going to be a matter of life or death."

I don't quite feel like I'm in a position of authority here, on my back, with a mouth full of my own blood and only the company of a one-wood at my side, but I have to question this.

"Don't you think you're exaggerating things just a little bit, Grampus? Life or death?"

He's still looking at the unfriendly skies. "Not a bit," he says. "Not one bit. You know what else? It's killing me a little bit right now, seeing you like this. Seeing you a loser." He taps his cane hard on the ground once, then three times more, his other hand shaking involuntarily in a weak half fist. He looks straighter up in the sky, bending almost backward, as if there, somehow, hides the true culprit. "We cannot keep losing all the time," he snaps.

Next thing I know, he is back at me, though not with words. He is poking me, first moderately, then hard, with his cane.

It hurts. It hurts in all the ways a thing can hurt, but mostly it hurts my heart, my spirit, to think what it means. As he continues jabbing me, a small groan of pain comes out of him with each poke. Like his pain, regardless, is worse than mine.

Then he's done. "I'm sorry," he says, and hobbles away quickly.

"It's okay," I say, hoping he will slow down or come back. It's sadder than sad, the desperate way he appears to be trying to run. But he doesn't slow down or come back.

I lie back flat and open my mouth wide in time to catch the first, purest egg-drop of rain as the clouds shed the storm that the heat has been promising for ages.

Maybe he is going crazy. But maybe I'm not helping.

Nobody wants to lose all the time. More important, nobody wants to *feel* like they're losing.

I must be lying there for a decent while because when I get up my clothes are soaked through, my hair is matted, and the taste of blood is replaced with clean and cool water. I am actually enjoying it, and when the first thundercrack rumbles the ground it just gets better.

I hear the splashes before I see the people, then the brothers Noblett come tearing around the end of the building, running in from the course to the club-house to get out of the weather. I am in exactly the spot they left me, and it must seem to them I haven't moved since I saw them last.

Right. I haven't.

Albie sails past me without a word. As his brother

waddles behind, like a big drenched rat with a golf bag, and tries to rush by, I grab him.

"Hold it, you," I say, thumping him against the building.

"Get off," he says. But I have a good grip of him.

"I've decided to play," I say.

Lightning sizzles across the sky. Thunder booms.

"Don't be an idiot," he says.

I keep him pinned. "Hey, it was your offer. Let's go play."

It is an excellent storm, the kind that brings Frankenstein's monster to life.

"What?" he says in a big tough voice that's not fooling anybody. "You think I'm afraid to go out there? You think I can't take a little weather?"

"That's what I think," I say.

"Let's go, rich boy," he says.

I think now when he says the word rich, the eyes are rolling back in both our heads. Mirror images.

By the time we reach the first tee, it is hard even to walk, we are so waterlogged. And the thunder and lightning are getting bigger, closer, angrier. Herb tees off, using my driver, and we can hardly see where the ball goes. I follow, and likewise hit one into nowhere.

No matter. It's the playing that counts, not the

game. We trudge on toward the hole, shortcutting, cheating, using extra balls to get through. But we get the hole completed. We do the same on the second, though just barely, and Herb practically cannot hit a ball because he is spending all his time looking up, when it lightnings, when it thunders, when it torments him with heavy quiet.

It looks like nighttime as we start up the hill. This is the one. The long steep climb to the open space atop the hill at the third tee.

Herb is in a full-blown panic. He is walking slower and slower as we take the hill. His neck is shrinking into his shoulders.

I'm carrying the bag now. And how do I feel?

On top of the world. Part of it is the sensation coming over me of exhilaration, like I'm getting charged directly from the electrical storm itself. There is nobody else in sight because there is nobody else daring, so the elements are all ours.

All mine, that is. Because Herb is not getting it, so he's not feeding off the elements like I am. I am getting stronger while he is getting weaker, and I have to confess how much I am loving that.

Invincible is what I feel right now. Untouchable. Beyond the reach of the things that can normally get to a person and bring him down.

Because I am doing this. I am doing something hard, and it feels important, even if to the outside world it might look stupid. It's winning, somehow, and it is bigger than winning.

"Hit me," Herb says, stopping right in front of me halfway up the hill. I practically walk right over him because I'm staring skyward as I go.

"What?" I say, staring into his rain-rivered face. He might even be crying.

"Hit me and we're even," he says. "Punch me in the mouth. Break my nose if that's what you want, but I'm not going any farther. This is insane. You are insane. That lightning is going to kill us."

I take it in, his fear and his offer, and I smile at him. I look up at the wicked wonderful sky and then back down at the wicked rotten in front of me.

"No, thank you," I say.

"Don't be stupid," he says. "It's a free shot. Who wouldn't take a free shot? I would, anybody would. Don't be lame."

I continue to smile. My split lip splits a little more. It hurts a little too, but here and now even this is a great feeling and the taste of my blood comes back like an old pal. With any luck I look like a ghoul to him now, in these conditions, blood running over my teeth.

"No," I say.

Thunder cracks at almost the same instant as the lightning blazes. It's really close now.

"Fine," Herb Noblett says. "Be an idiot. Keep the club. Be a freak."

"Thank you, I will," I say.

He grabs for the bag, but I yank it away.

"I said I was going to play my game," I say, "and I am. I'll need these. If you don't trust me with your clubs, you can caddy for me and watch them."

He is already running down the hill.

"You have mental problems," Herb says, wheeling wildly away.

"We call it drain bamage in my family," I say, and turn to take the rest of the hill to the third hole.

It does indeed feel like the top of the world when I get to the tee. The top of a wild, wild world with the wind blowing hard and the rain pounding me all over. And I feel very much like the king of this world.

I hit a drive with the wind at my back, and it rockets off into the sky, traveling maybe miles, from the way it feels. I cannot see it, of course, but I'm looking off after it anyway, holding the pose of my perfect follow-through, savoring the moment, when the biggest explosion of thunder shakes the ground below me. Lightning zaps from the distance, across the fields, straight in my direction, looking for all the world like it's got my name on it, until it snaps back away like the snap of a cosmic cowboy whip.

I put my big Slazenger Anti-Slice club back into the bag. I run headlong down that hill toward the clubhouse so hard, the sounds of the clubs and my bones rattling are interchangeable.

But I'm laughing all the same. Because I am winning. We are winning.

13

IT'S ONLY A GAME

You can't take things lying down. You can't just let things happen to you, or they will. And you'll be a loser.

"I thought this was going to be the sweetest summer of my life, Grammus."

"I hear you," she says. "So did I. I'm supposed to be back at the pool in Florida by now, splashing around with a bunch of Dolphins. Maxie's already back down there, and I'm sure he's using up all the sunshine."

She twists her upper body halfway around, then snaps it back in the other direction like she's spring-loaded. She hits a wicked drive that launches like a rocket and violently breaks up a meeting of seagulls in the field around the pin 150 yards away.

I believe my grandmother is the finest athlete I have ever seen up close.

"I didn't think everything was going to turn all serious and everything was going to come back to money," I say.

"Everything is serious, and everything comes back to money," she says.

"You see, I don't understand, then. If you think that, why do you seem to be having such fun all the time no matter what you're doing?"

"Simple," she says. "Because I *have* money."

This is depressing. Not just because I don't have money, which I don't. But because it is an explanation that does not get me any closer to working out the key to ultimate happiness. Because Grammus is the happiest, most successful person in the vicinity, and she says it's all down to dough, so you kind of have to believe her.

Except, I don't.

"Come on, Grammus, that's not true. You don't believe that."

"No," she says, "you're right. The real key has more to do with my very healthy sex life. But I thought you might prefer that I spared you that."

"Money," I call out just before I swing wildly and

drive a ball straight and hard and right into the trees. "Money it is. Got it. Key to happiness. No need to expand on that. Thanks anyway. Money."

She comes over and puts an arm around my shoulders. I feel like pulling away at first because knowing that my grandmother has a sex life, not to mention a *healthy* one, is kind of putting me off physical contact of any kind. But the feeling passes in an instant because in her strong, warm squeeze, this is my grammus who pushed me on the swings for hours, who struck me out so many times at Wiffle ball I threw the bat on top of the garage, who tackled me face-first into the grass when we were only supposed to be playing tag football. Whatever she did with herself since then could never undo the greatness of her.

As long as I didn't think about it.

"Listen, Jock, the thing is, money cannot make you happy, but it can make you pretty damn sad. Your parents, for example, have a lovely attitude to money, while your grandfather, historically, has not."

"I know. But even since he changed, after his stroke, he doesn't seem all that happy. He just sits in that golf cart like it's a wheelchair. It's depressing."

"Well, physical activity is important too. For the head. I don't know where I'd be if I couldn't play golf.

Which, by the way, *you* cannot. My dear grandson, I love you to pieces, but you are so abysmal at this, I believe every time you swing a club, somebody in Scotland drops down dead."

"I know. Grampus likes me playing, though."

"I know, that's why I'm here now. I'm supposed to be coaching you. He's engaged me as your pro. Do you even like playing?"

"Nope. I do it for him. He wants me to be a player. I like the driving range, though. I'm happy to go there every day."

"Then do that. Lots of people only own one club, the driver. The driving range is a great thing. And it keeps the hackers like you from chopping up the grass and ruining everything for the rest of us."

"And I'd like to oblige. But . . ."

"The old man. Well, have you tried telling him?"

"Yup."

"Hmm," she says. "Come with me."

He's been watching us, of course. He can hardly be discreet, the way he wheels around the place in his cart, humming and buzzing, then coming to a sudden stop to watch whatever needs watching. He can be there for hours at a time in one place, just staring. Then he mysteriously zips away to plant himself somewhere else. He can turn up in the middle of a fairway where you have to be careful not to plunk him in the noggin with your drive, or on the top of a hill a quarter-mile away, looking down over us like a little motorized shepherd. We find him right now "speeding" his way across the gravel parking lot toward his workshop, where he was going to hide and pretend he wasn't staring.

"Gus," Grammus calls.

He drives a little faster. It's barely detectable, but he has accelerated as he guns it for the safety of his workshop. We follow in hot pursuit—walking—as he parks his machine and hobbles with his cane into the workshop. I don't even know why he's being so goofy, but he is right now one goofy little man.

It's like an old garage, halfway between a garage and a barn. The two ancient wooden doors that face onto the parking lot have a row of windows at eye level, set into rotting old frames. Grammus peeks in just ahead of me, then turns.

"We'll give him a minute or two, to compose himself for company," she says.

I nudge past her and take a peek in, and I see my grandfather, leaning hunched close to a mirror that hangs on the far wall. He is working hard and frantic, pawing at his comb-over as if the high-speed chase in the golf cart has disturbed hairs that haven't been disturbed since they were shellacked in place two days ago.

I pull away from the window and face my grandmother. She is wearing the kind of smile that is definitely a smile, even though it's curving downward, an expression covering all the bases.

"He is a vain man, your grandfather."

"By vain, you mean great, right?"

Her smile tips all the way back up. "I do."

We've given him plenty of composure time, and we ease our way into the workshop. He has flumped himself down into his chair and is hunched over his work area as if he has been hard at inventing the next big thing.

But it's clear as soon as Grammus taps his shoulder and turns him around, his biggest thing is not on his desk at all.

"Hiya, Helen," he says, the working half of his mouth going all goofy grin while the other half hangs flat.

"Hiya, Gus," she says.

"I want to thank you again, for taking on the project here. He's going to be great, isn't he?"

"Well, first off, he is my grandson too, after all, so it's no imposition. And second of all, he may very well be a great in time, but it won't be at golf."

"Why? What do you mean?"

"He can't golf, Gus."

"Of course he can. He can and he will. He's the dream, he's the hope. Aren't you, Jock? Aren't you the dream and the hope? Tell her."

This, I have to say, takes me way by surprise. Not that he still thought I could play some, but that he thought I could really *play.* And that he cared so much.

I thought all the delusion had left him. I thought that when the stroke came in it bumped all the truly mad dream stuff out. I thought that peculiar region of his brain had died.

This must be the only part of his modest little life dream left. Am I supposed to kill it for good?

"Jock?" he asks.

I swear, I feel like I am answering him. I swear, my body feels like it is vibrating with sound, muffled sound like when you block your own ears when you're speaking, but sound.

But it's not. Grampus stares at me and waits for me and waits until there is nothing to wait for anymore. Then his eyes fade right there in front of me, the light paling right out of them like they're on a dimmer switch. He swerves around in his chair and shows us his hunchy back.

"It's only a game," I blurt. "What are you doing? It's only a game. You're not supposed to be crazy anymore, and you're not supposed to care about stupid stuff like this. After the stroke, after getting rid of the digger and the snooker table and the visions of unlimited wealth and luxury and all that were wiped away, you were on the better side of things, and I liked you a lot better on the better side. You have the best life of anybody I know, Grampus, and it seems to me you are the only person who doesn't know that. I don't want the PGA pro tour life. You know what life I want? I want *yours*, ya daffy old man."

I'm looking at my mighty grandfather now, or looking at his tense little back as he fusses and struggles over some small silly something on his worktable, and I feel like some kind of snake. He won't respond. He could be holding his breath, or crying, or writing his memoirs for all I can tell.

So what. It was right. I was right. It is about winning and losing and the only thing worse than being a loser is being a winner who *thinks* he's always losing.

It's only a game, for cripes' sake. It doesn't matter. None of any of it matters. I thought he knew that now.

Grammus turns my way and gives me an okay nod and a blink that does not in any way make me feel quite okay but thanks for trying. She scoots up closer to him, peeking over his low shoulder as he tries to make some alteration to his already badly altered game of not-baseball with the square ball. He's growling his frustration sound.

"What is it you're doing here, then, Gus?" she asks sweetly.

He pauses. Whatever it is he's got there—his Exacto knife or big tailor's shears or some such—he is getting flustered as it clearly fails to do what he wants it to. He slams down the Exacto knife or the big shears or whatever and grabs his cane as Grammus steps briskly back. He takes the cane and starts smashing, smashing, small human figures and walls and carefully laid bits of terrain in his mock-up playing field, smashing further, the mirror on the wall, knocking over the box of artisan's tools and paints and rulers and draftsman's gear ranged around his beloved and perfectly tended workstation where he has spent a good portion of his latter life.

When the dust has settled, the dust of the racket no longer drifting down over us, he regains his manners and answers Grammus's question.

"Nothing," he says as if just exactly that, nothing, has just happened. "It's nothing, Helen."

He turns his chair around to face us again, leans on his cane like he's about to tell a charming nonviolent old duffer story.

"Will you remarry me?" he asks her, with a sweetness you could not fake and all the hope in the world on his face.

"Um, Jock?" Grammus says without looking at me, "could you excuse us? You can go to the driving range or something while your grandfather and I straighten up in here."

14

RUNNING THE TABLE

"Bingo? *Bingo?!*"

Egon is not well-pleased.

"So?" I say. "What's so wrong with bingo?"

"Bingo? On the very spot where the sacred snooker once was played? Are you serious? That's like pulling down Fenway Park and putting in a *library*."

"What's wrong with libraries?" I ask.

"See? See?" he says, stomping his way toward what used to be the rumpus room and is now the bingo palace. "There's no reasoning with you."

We enter the room, and it has certainly been transformed. Where the table once was—the gargantuan, vast green football-field of a snooker table—there is now a sea of cottony white heads, floating above cards on tables, poised for the fight. There are six circular tables of four players spread about the area, all splayed in the congregation of their bingo god. The Caller.

You wouldn't even think these people had faces. The game has not started, but they all have their heads so low and serious on the tabletops that you would swear there was some rational way of figuring out the angles in advance of the starter's gun. As if they really think it is something they can tweak, like baseball, rather than a total crapshoot, like the lottery.

But when the star, The Caller, gets going, things take a twist. It goes from mere prize draw to Las Vegas–style *event*.

"You see?" Egon says as we take our spots in front of the two remaining cards at the back of the room nearest the door. "You see what they've done here?"

"Hell-looo, ladies . . . !"

It's Carlo. Carlo has a job, finally, and it is playing scaly game show host to a room full of Grampus's disappointed old girlfriends. The truth is, they already lost the biggest *bingo* of them all when Grampus started dating Grammus again, and we should probably fly in the equally disappointed 1972 Miami Dolphins and get them together.

The prizes, written on a blackboard mounted on the wall where the pool cue rack used to hang, aren't likely to make the ladies any more satisfied. It's all stuff they used to get anyway—free golf cart morning, round of golf, complimentary meal for two in the protein-free café—except with the deduction of one dashing combed-over codger who will remain nameless. So Carlo's required to sell it all with his charm.

"Hey," he says, pointing at a lady in the front table, "I bet you used to be *hot,* a long time ago in a galaxy far, far away."

Turns out, it's Carlo's dream to be a stand-up comic some day. I guess since they usually wind up as game show hosts, he's fast-tracking.

He spins the tub that juggles the balls that carry the letters and numbers of the ladies' tired little dreams. And he joyfully mocks them. "You know, that would be a beautiful hairdo on somebody else . . . B-six . . ."

"God, it's so awful already," I say.

"Shut up," Egon says, "I got B-six."

"Oh jeez, what do you want to win, a round of golf? You can play all you want as it is."

"I don't want to use it, dingleberry, I want to sell it to somebody else."

"Glad you're back, Egon. You're a great addition to the staff."

"Thanks. Shut up."

"O-twenty-four. Egon?" Carlo shouts out, "The O is the one that looks like a doughnut."

The bingo ladies all turn around to laugh hysterically at my brother, who looks up from his card and stares with a combination of horror and menace at each one individually. The bingo ladies are unmoved and laugh more.

Bingo is more fun than I gave it credit for.

"But that doesn't mean you can eat the card," Carlo adds, wagging a finger. "Remember, Egon, no eating the card. You might want to write that on your hand, *Egon no eat doughnut card . . .*"

The ladies love it. Carlo was born for the bingo circuit, and is such a hit my sister may have something to worry about here.

Egon handles the setback with the good grace and sportsmanship that he handles most things. He swipes *my* card and all my markers right off the table and onto the floor. Then he takes his own card and, jumping to his feet, sails it like a deadly Frisbee at the master of ceremonies. Carlo is having far too good a time to notice, and takes the corner of the card right in the eye.

"Bingo!" Egon shouts as Carlo covers up and doubles over.

Egon, for his troubles, is now getting booed. I have never seen anything quite like it, outside of my dreams, where he is in fact booed all the time, as well as being blasted with fire hoses, dragged behind galloping horses, and fed to a gang of tiny cannibals who all look just like him. But this is even better, as he shouts back at all the old ladies booing him and throwing little bingo chips that, admittedly, aren't exactly bullets coming his way. Can't have everything.

"Did you see that in there?" he says as we tumble out of the former rumpus room. He's livid. I can't see a whole lot of anything because I am crying with laughter. "I'm going to tell Meredith," he says, storming toward the front desk.

"That's an excellent idea," I say, trotting after him.

"Blah-hah-hah-hah," Meredith laughs, even louder than me. There are few sights in this world more heartwarming than Egon in a fury. "Carlo said those things? My Carlo? Jeez, I was thinking of dumping him, but now I think I need to catch his act first."

I can hear laughter all over the complex at this moment. It is as if the whole operation has been transformed from a place with barely a pulse to a hot spot that could give Foxwoods Casino a run for its money.

"You know what you've done?" I say to Egon as I follow along on his victory tour of the new regime.

"What have I done, jerk?"

"You have brought joy. Joy, I tell you. Do you hear the sound of laughter wherever you go around here? It is a miracle, and you are responsible."

"Shut up," he says, rushing to the café and the safety of his mother's unconditional love. "I have done no such thing. Don't say that. I have brought no joy to any of you dingleberries."

As it happens, Peach is already in the process of laughing before Mr. Funstuff even reaches her. The café is empty, except for herself, seated at a table, and Genghis the cat.

"What is he doing here?" Egon demands.

"He's here for food," Peach says happily. She giggles some more as the big-head cat paws at her leg.

"He is supposed to feed himself. That's what he's here for. Make him go out and kill something."

"Kill something?" Peach says. "Not *my* baby. He wouldn't hurt a thing."

"Yes he would," Egon insists. "That's what he's designed for. He *likes* hurting things."

"I think you're confusing yourself with the animal," I say. "Honest mistake."

"Anyway," Peach says, "this pussycat isn't hurting anything. He's a vegetarian."

"No he is *not*," Egon snaps, appalled at the sudden decrease of bloodlust in the world.

"Sure he is," she says. "Watch."

My mother reaches into her smock and pulls out a handful of . . . beans? She starts feeding them to Genghis one by one, the way you would feed sugar lumps to a horse. And in fact he gobbles them like a horse.

"Red kidney beans," Peach says proudly. "He comes around every afternoon just begging for them. It's awfully cute."

"What about the mouse?" I ask.

"Oh, you know about the mouse."

"Of course," Egon says, "that's what we brought Genghis in for, to rip the mouse's little head off."

Peach scowls at him. "Are you telling me that you bought this wonderful creature just to be an assassin?"

"Yup," he says proudly, "and you even helped us, remember?"

"Well then, I'm happy to report that the mouse is

getting along just fine. In fact, I told Genghis that he could keep him. He lives in the gap under your grandfather's workshop, and we feed him there every afternoon and he knows he's not to come in the kitchen. He's a very good boy, just like Genghis. And, likewise, a vegetarian."

As you could imagine, all of this is just like poking Egon with a big stick.

"Why do you talk like this, Peach?" Egon says. "You know it only upsets me. You can't tell a mouse to stay outside. You can't tell a cat he can have a pet mouse. You cannot turn carnivores into vegetarians."

"You see," she says gently, more gently as he gets more flustered, "it's all in the way you handle them. You have to talk to them sweetly, and with respect, and then you get respect back. And once they stop eating other living creatures, you find that the peaceable side of their natures comes naturally through. I am hoping we can work the same wonders with you over time." Her voice has dropped to a peaceable whisper, sending him into a spasm of rage.

"That does it. We are going to get this place back in shape no matter what it takes. We are bringing money, and meat, and snooker back into this operation and then it'll be right side up again. Come on, Jock," he says, stalking off, "let's go eat a sheep."

Peach beckons for me to stay.

"He does get himself worked up, doesn't he?"

"Ya," I say, "it was great."

"The thing is, we have got money coming in. The business is doing quite well now. I don't think there are that many golfers around, but we seem to be doing a brisk business, anyway."

"Bingo and bean paste," I say.

"Bingo and bean paste indeed," she says. "So, your father and I were talking and decided that in a way Egon is quite right—"

"Don't *say* that."

"Not about meat, certainly. We've got the karma just right in here now and nobody is going to interfere with that. But with the money we thought it would be nice to go and buy back Grampus's snooker table, as a surprise."

"Really?" I ask, a little surprised at my own enthusiasm. "Because, to tell you the truth, as much fun as the bingo seems to be providing right now, it's kind of a lot less cool than the pool table was. I was seeing my perfect summer as something kind of different before, compared to what it's become."

Although what it's become is pretty amazing in

itself. My parents, as out-of-spacey as they are, must be on to something with the whole karma notion because against all the odds they have created the humming, buzzing, whistling customer-magnet Grampus always wanted but couldn't quite manage. That's life being funny, I guess, in a way my grandfather would not find amusing.

"Well, the bingo isn't going anywhere, because it's been a big hit. But I think there is enough room here to accommodate a variety of pastimes for a variety of customers. Spice of life and all that, you know."

"And hamburgers."

"Not hamburgers, no."

I head out with a new sense of purpose and a feeling of rightness as I get on my bike. I am to ride over to Fame&Fortune, meet up with Leonard, and travel on over to Teddy's to try and bring the fabled table back home. This is possibly the highlight of what has turned out to be an eventful, weird summer. If we can pull off this transaction, it comes kind of close to making life here at the complex as perfect as I had always hoped it would be. We are, miraculously, making money now under the shrewd business leadership of my freak-o hippy parents, and while there have had to be some compromises (a shortage of meat and meat by-products, an overabundance of people with hair like cotton who have too much free time and enthusiasm for handing out advice to a young rube like me), there have been undeniable improvements (success). Bringing back the snooker table represents a triumph, a big green victory cigar that celebrates the blending of the old-time sports paradise that the complex once was with the slightly goofy but financially stable social club it now is.

Almost too good to be true, but a lovely mongrel of a place it is, and a temple to the notion that maybe the key to attaining wealth and success is not to give a monkey's about the attainment of wealth and success.

My grandfather's term for this would be idiot's luck.

I am up to about fifteen miles per hour, streaking out of the parking lot when it strikes. Sailing just across my vision and into my front wheel comes an old duffel bag, brown canvas and beat, the one we use to haul old equipment around. The one Egon has used to master the maneuver of throwing a rider from a bike.

The bag slaps precisely into the front wheel, wraps itself, then turns over until it jams up between the wheel and the frame. As the wheel freezes, the rest of the bike and the rider continue on as momentum and nature intended. Up and over I go, soaring over the handlebars like I've been catapulted.

Having been through this a number of times before, I manage, during flight, to look over in the direction of the perpetrator and watch his oily smile as I crash shoulder-first to the rough and rugged ground.

I am lying there, groaning, pressed to the ground, when he comes over.

"Where you going?" he says so casually it makes me shudder.

"Fame&Fortune," I say.

He looks at me more closely, to make sure I'm okay, of course.

"You don't need a haircut," he says. "You might need a Band Aid, though."

"What's going on?" Grampus asks, tooling up in his golf cart.

"Jock fell down," Egon says. "I was helping him."

The old guy is not quite that out of it. "I don't see why anyone should need help falling down," Grampus says. As he pulls up, he reaches out with his walking stick and starts poking Egon sharply, shooing him away like chasing scavengers off a not-quite-dead carcass.

"What are you characters up to?" Grampus asks.

"I'm getting the hose, to flood underneath your workshop, to kill a rodent," Egon says. "It'll be fun. Want to do it with me?"

"Not me," Grampus says, "I'm busy planning a party."

"Pretty much the same thing," Egon says.

"Quiet, you," I say, getting to my feet. I pull at the duffel bag wrapped tight in my front wheel. It is well stuck. "What's the party for, Grampus?"

"Employee of the Month. Don't tell anyone, but it's your grandmother, and I have a very special gift for her."

"Hey," I say, "I didn't get a party when I won."

"Yes," he says, an unwelcome twinkle in his yellow eye, "well she has gone above and beyond the call of duty."

"Arrggh," Egon says, making a little cross with his index fingers like Grampus is Dracula, "I think I'm gonna be sick."

This pleases Grampus even more. He is enjoying his role as randy old scamp. I would be just as happy about this making my brother sick if I weren't getting a little queasy myself.

"Ya, looks like we all have important chores to tend to, Grampus," I say. I get Egon to pull the bag in one direction while I pull the bike the other way.

Grampus shakes his head at me. "Don't you know what's about to happen, Jock?"

I look at him while continuing to pull mightily. "What?" I ask.

I get my answer in a fraction of a second, as Egon lets go of his end and I go bouncing on my backside, my bike reversing itself right into my chest before keeling over on its side.

"You're really going to need to get wise to the darker side of life there, Jock," Grampus says, putting off again in his clown car.

"I am my own worst enemy," I say.

"That's stupid," Egon says, laughing, "I am." But he's laughing kind of sadly because I am such a disappointment. "It's not like you don't have enough exposure to it."

"You're not as bad as you seem," I say, just to get him back, since I have nothing else.

"D'ya love me?" he says, hands on hips like the Jolly Green Jerk.

Of course, once Egon hears the top-secret mission I am going on, even drowning a mouse loses all its glamour. He's dying to get back to Teddy's place, and dying even more to get the pool table back.

"You leave everything to me," Egon says as we cycle to the barbershop. "Between you and Leonard, the whole deal will go belly-up in a second. I speak Teddy's language."

"Teddy speaks grunt?" I ask, just managing to accelerate out of kickshot.

It is a truly historic meeting. Like Stalin and Roosevelt getting together during World War II to sort everything out nice before their countries spend fifty years throwing rocks at each other. My father and Teddy come from as opposite sides of the money/lifestyle/personal philosophy world as you can get. For example, things get off to a bad start when Leonard leans his ancient Schwinn mailman's bike up against Teddy's gleaming Jaguar.

My dad isn't careless about people's stuff. He just doesn't care about it. If you know what I mean.

"Hey," Egon snaps, lifting the bike right off. It is a huge tall thing, this bike, so tall Leonard can't reach the ground without tipping it way to one side. It looks like a circus thing as Egon wheels it away, the crossbar around his chin. "Bad enough you had to bring this goofy thing and embarrass us all over the place. Do you have to let it attack all the nicer stuff too?"

"That car is not nicer than my bicycle," Leonard says gallantly.

"Oh jeez, Len," Egon says, covering his face like a criminal in the newspaper and hustling Leonard to the door. "You might as well be wearing a hat with a little propeller on it."

We walk straight through the front door without knocking or anything. It's Teddy's office, but it looks like somebody's house, so it feels like we should be knocking. Teddy is, among other things, a real estate developer, and his office is the corner building on a huge development of new three-, four-, and five-bedroom homes. It is, in fact, the show home that tells all prospective buyers just how plush and wonderful life in a TeddyHome (yes, that's what he calls them) will be. As we step in through the front door, it seems life here would be pretty plush and wonderful indeed.

"Kid," Teddy says, popping up from his desk in what would be the living room. "How the hell are ya?"

He doesn't mean me. He rushes over and gives Egon the kind of embrace that means either one of them just hit a grand slam in the World Series, or he's going to have him killed. "I wondered when you'd be back. The place is a lot duller without you around."

"Of course," Egon says, "like every place."

"And you brought the team," Teddy says, shaking Leonard's hand energetically and punching my shoulder with his free meaty fist.

"Hello, Teddy," Leonard says. "Lovely place you have here."

"You like it? I've got two thousand others just like it."

"Thanks anyway," Leonard says politely, proudly, "but I already have a home."

"Is it a TeddyHome?"

"I don't think it is. But it's nice."

"It's too small," Egon spouts.

"It is not, it's just right," I say.

"Casa Dingleberry," Egon says.

Teddy is a busy man. "So, then, you didn't come to buy a house."

"No, actually," Leonard says awkwardly. Leonard is no part businessman. Haggling and dealmaking do not come naturally. "We came to buy something else."

"Sure," Teddy says, slapping my father on both shoulders at once. "What do you need? Guns? Plutonium? A case of nice Danish hams?"

Poor Leonard is way over his head here. "Oh my,

no. We don't want anything evil. We just want to buy back my father's pool table from you."

"Snooker," Teddy chirps.

"Snooker," Leonard chirps back even chirpier.

"No," Teddy says.

So, that went well.

Leonard never saw it coming. "No? Is that what you said?"

"It is." Teddy says in a bouncy tone that sounds more like he not only said *yes*, but also refused to let us pay for it, and insisted on putting it on his back right now and delivering it himself. "Listen, guys, come with me."

Teddy puts a big arm over Egon's shoulders and leads us through the living room, over lush brown carpeting so thick and squashy there could be a layer of whipped cream underneath, to the back of the house and around to the dining room, with big French doors opening onto a velvety green quarter-acre lawn.

"You coming back to work for me?" he asks Egon.

"Yup," Egon says.

The dining room does not have a dining table. It has a vintage snooker table. Teddy racks 'em up and hands a cue to Leonard to break.

"He doesn't mean for you to actually *break* it, Leonard . . ." I say.

"I do know that much, Jock," he says, though it is entirely possible he did not know that. Regardless, he doesn't know much more than that about the game, and the result is tough going.

Leonard breaks, barely. The cue ball squigs off the tip of the stick and hardly bothers the giggling collection of balls triangled in the middle of the felt.

Leonard stares at the balls just lying there. "Why can't you sell us back the table, Teddy?"

Teddy goes about the business of shooting and actually striking balls as he answers. "Because that's not how the game is played, Leonard." He cracks off a shot that sounds like a small caliber pistol when the balls collide. Balls rocket into holes here and there as if they are afraid to remain on the table a second longer. He lines up another shot.

"I don't get it," Leonard says. "You can play the game however you want to play it. You can have any table you want."

"I want this one," he says, ripping off another perfect, successful shot. He looks like if he weren't dominating the real estate world, he could be a professional pool player. "If I just turned around and gave you back this table, which I treasure, then where would I be?"

"You'd be wherever you want to be," my father rightly points out. "You're the kind of guy who can have and do whatever he wants. My father loves this table, Teddy, you know that. And you are his friend."

"I am his friend. That's one more reason I have to say no. He knows as well as I do that this is the way the game is played."

"What game are you talking about? Is it pool? Because if it's pool, I think it's pretty obvious you could successfully play a great game of pool on a Ping-Pong table."

It's true, he's amazing. Through the whole conversation he keeps shooting away, hardly even slowing down when he shoots.

Running the table is what it's called. Every shot he takes goes in and entitles him to another shot, which he makes, and another. The other guy never even gets a chance.

Egon stares at Teddy with his mouth hanging open, unfortunately falling more under Teddy's spell than ever.

"I'm talking about the big game, Leonard, The Big Game of Everything."

"You already *have* everything, Teddy. What more

could somebody like you possibly need?"

"That's just the point, Leonard. I do have everything. You can only drive so many cars, eat so many meals, right? But you know, you find out when you get where I've gotten that there *is* more. There's lots more. Only you don't know what it is."

Egon cuts in. "I'm confused. Is there more? Is there not more? Are we getting the table?"

Teddy laughs. "I do love having you around, boy. And that is the only way you will be playing on this table, because it is staying right here. It's a special table, it's a great table. I have it, and somebody else doesn't. That's a double. That makes me happy. That makes me a little farther up in the Big Game of Everything."

Egon is enthralled with this turn of information. "Can I play the Big Game of Everything? How do I get in?"

"Stick with me, lad, and I'll show you."

Leonard, with great dignity and control, lays down his arms. He takes his pool cue and places it right down on the table, in between the white cue ball and the black eight ball Teddy is about to sink in the far corner. Teddy is crouched low over the shot, then looks up at Leonard with a grin. "Excuse me," he says, "but I need to get this shot to win the game."

Leonard, with maybe a little less dignity, takes the ball and stuffs it into the pocket with his hand. "Well, you won't be getting that shot," he says, his voice rising and thinning. "And you won't be getting this *boy*, either." He grabs Egon by the hand and marches him toward the front door.

"Why won't he be getting me?" Egon protests. "I want him to get me. I want to be in the Big Game of Everything."

Leonard does not answer him but continues on, hauling him to the front door. It is the most physically assertive thing I have ever seen him do. This is Leonard enraged, and I am flat-out stunned by him. I, just like everybody who has ever met him, love my father. He is as soft and warm and unusual a creature as God has ever coughed up. But if I am honest, I have to tell you that I have not always seen the strength of my father, toughness or a can-do attitude. Part of me always kind of thought he was a softie because he had no choice in the matter.

I thought Grampus was the tough one and Leonard was the pushover.

I jump as Leonard bursts back in through the door, his face redder than I have ever seen it, and storms right up to Teddy. The world is dangerously upended all of a sudden.

"You are not my father's friend," Leonard says, breathing lentil-breath-of-fire right up Teddy's nose. "You are no longer welcome at the golf club. If you come there, I cannot be held accountable for my actions." He is shaking. Leonard, that is. Teddy's pretty calm. I can hear my father's tense, excited breathing from across the room. "I'm sorry," he adds in a high, angry snort.

He's sorry. The cherry on top. Leonard getting all feisty and loyal and defensive of the old man, then apologizing at the end of it.

I have to remember not to overlook my father's greatness.

I myself am left standing against the wall in the room with Teddy and the table. I guess I was not considered *at risk* of falling into his clutches like my brother.

"Guess I'll be going," I say.

"See you around," Teddy says.

Inspired by Leonard's championship performance, I figure I'll go for it. "So, will we just take the table with us, or would you like to send it along?"

He stares at me, blinks.

It was worth a shot. I walk out in the still-hot vapor trail of my macho hippy father's outrage. Leonard makes an art of seeing the good of humanity, even when it's not really there, so this was a hit and I feel bad for him, but at the same time I feel, *Go, Leonard*. I don't think even Grampus would mind as much what just happened because, like Teddy said, the old man understands as well as anyone how the game is and is not played.

But this, as I step out the door into a further setback, tops everything.

"Grammus?" I say, a little surprised.

Like two pairs of gunfighters squared off against each other, Leonard and Egon are standing rigid, facing Grammus and Lukas.

"We were just coming to play a little pool," she says.

"Ma?" Leonard says in a befuddled voice.

"What?" she asks, pretty much the same way. "I'm just out having a little fun. Can't a lady have a little fun now and then?"

"What about Dad?" Leonard asks. "And for that matter, what happened to Maxie?"

"Nothing happened to Maxie. I'm meeting him back in Florida next week. As for your father, I've been having fun with him too. In fact, I'd say I've been making him a very happy chappy, so what's the problem?"

Not sure I like where we're heading with this.

"It's getting iffy in here," I say to Egon. "You wanna just cycle off?"

It's like he hasn't even heard me. "You just get to do, like, whatever you want?" he says to our popular and energetic grandmother. And if it sounds at all like a criticism, well, it isn't.

"Of course I do, dear, I am a woman of mature years. I should do whatever I want, don't you think?"

"I do," Egon says. The competition for Egon's number one role model has just heated up. "You are *so* cool, Grammus."

"So they say," she says.

I'm guessing Grampus isn't one of *they*.

"I don't think Dad was thinking it was all for laughs," Leonard says to Grammus.

She pauses. She knows what Leonard is saying is true, even if she does try and pretend everything is cool and nothing really matters. You can see it in the way she slices her eyes, right then left, that she's not entirely onboard for her own story. She takes a step toward Leonard, who as we know is taking no prisoners or nonsense this afternoon.

He puts up a hand to keep her where she is. "You think maybe you're being a little . . . careless?" he asks.

Now she looks away with her whole body. She turns around like she's leaving, then turns back to face him again.

I have never seen her look like this. Unsure. Underpowered. She suddenly looks less like a first lady or a retired athlete, more like a slightly frail elder lady. "I thought I would bring a little joy to his life, for a little while. Seemed like it was in short supply."

Since nobody who knew anything could argue with that, nobody says anything for a minute. We are one awkward bunch, I have to say. My father, my brother, my grandmother, and her date, who is one of my grandfather's oldest friends, standing around discussing . . . my grandfather, whose beloved snooker table is behind us in the very successful office of his other squintillionaire best buddy, who also happens to be playing that table like it has never been played before. Even the table is probably happier in its new home. All the while Grampus himself, the straw that is stirring this particular cocktail, is back at his complex. He's not even here, and he's taking an absolute

] 254 [

drubbing in the Big Game of Everything.

"You know, you are Employee of the Month for August," I say to Grammus because I want her in the picture.

"I am?" she says, at first tickled but then cluing in. "Oh. Oh."

"You're not supposed to know. There are decorations going up, and a big prize and everything."

"Oh," she says again.

Leonard has run out of things to say. It's part of being Leonard that if you don't have anything nice to say then you don't say anything, and he *always* has something nice to say. Not that there is anything nasty to say, either, but I think he's just sad. He gets on his bike.

"So I guess we'll see you at the celebration," I tell her.

She smiles weakly and walks past us into the office for her game of snooker.

And Lukas follows silently, going after two of Grampus's biggest trophies and scoring about a trillion Big Game of Everything points as he does.

15

GAME ON

Things slip into a kind of suspended animation for a few days. It really is the wind-down part of the summer, and you can feel it. It is still summer hot, but you can smell the end of vacation and the beginning of school coming right around the corner. Meredith is so ready to go off to college that she only shows up to work one day out of three, spends half of those days disappearing with Carlo the bingo king, and doesn't really appear to know the rest of us very well at all.

Mostly though, right now, things are suspended in Grampus time. Grammus hasn't been by the last several days, so the spark she brought to the complex and its owner has fizzled into nothing. The big August celebration of Employee of the Month has been stuck in the starting gate waiting for the actual worker to show herself and collect her prize, never mind actually work.

There is a picture of Grammus the size of a big flag hanging on the wall above all the classic golf guys. She is posing at the first tee, smiling and leaning on her driver like she's about to kick into a tap dance routine.

Grampus acts a little more like a psychiatric patient every day. He walks back and forth between the office and the workshop. He looks anxious when he comes in the main door. He looks flattened a few seconds later when he trudges off again. He wears his shirt all the time, and his shoes, so for sure he is taking no pleasure out of the remaining summer sunshine.

He looks like he's making the long walk from death row to the executioner, over and over and over again.

"Get over it," Egon says as we sit in the golf cart and watch him go back and forth. "He only wanted her back for the money, anyway."

"No, no," I say, "that's not it at all. That was *you*. He wanted her back for love, not money."

He looks puzzled, but inquisitive. "Does that really happen in real life?"

"It happens to actual human beings, yes."

"Huh," he says. "That's something. You know, I was surprised Teddy didn't let us have the table back. But you can see his point."

"His point is, there is no honor among thieves."

"So? Who needs honor when you're allowed to steal? And besides, he bought the table, he didn't steal it."

"It's an expression. And, in spirit, he stole it. It doesn't rightly belong to him, or to Lukas. Neither does the cart. Neither does the digger."

"Okay, then you want to steal it all back?"

"What is it with you? You don't care whose side you're on, as long as it's the side that's doing all the nasty stuff?"

"Hey, maybe I'm just always on the side of the underdog, ever think of that?"

"No."

He laughs. "Ya, you were right the first time."

"Right. Whatever, it hardly matters, since there's no way of getting Grampus's stuff back no matter what kind of scheme you come up with."

At that moment, just as Grampus shuts the door behind him after his latest snail trudge into his workshop, the whole point becomes pointless anyway. The same flatbed truck that took his toys away is now bringing them back, pulling up and settling right in the middle of the parking lot. The golf cart is there, with the digger parked right behind it. The snooker table, however, is not part of the package.

Down from the cab of the truck hop Lukas and Grammus, both of them all smiles. They march straight into the clubhouse, leaving the delivery sitting there.

"What is this all about?" I say, hopping out of the golf cart and heading over.

"It's about the Big Game of Everything," Egon says, bounding past me, "and we're winning again."

He scrambles up onto the flatbed and puts himself right into the control seat of the digger. He's bouncing up and down and pretending to work the controls, like a little kid with his Tonka trucks at the beach. I leave him there and walk into the office.

Grammus is standing there, staring up at her big picture hovering over the whole of the world. Her eyes are wide and bright as golf balls, and both of her hands cover her mouth.

"Nope," Lukas is saying happily to my shocked mother who is working the counter. "I don't want a thing. Not a penny." Lukas is enjoying himself in that way that people do when they are sharing three Doritos with you because they have twelve bags in the car.

Peach is tickled. Not that she could possibly care one bit less about golf carts or diggers or cold cash, because she couldn't. Possession of any kind, of any thing, means nothing to her and she would be happiest if everybody just agreed to trade smiles and good deeds for whatever they needed and we all joined hands around a roaring campfire of all the world's legal currency. She has no pride, false or otherwise, about taking whatever tainted graciousness Lukas is peddling here as long as somebody is probably going to come out happier from it. Grampus, the somebody in this case.

"Well, at least let me get you a bowl of my lovely borscht, and maybe some kasha."

"That would be a great deal," Lukas says, "if I hadn't just eaten."

The bell rings on the front door, and everyone looks to see the gaunt, grim proprietor walk in. Grammus takes her hands down from her mouth, but holds on to the whole rest of her startled expression. If Grampus registers the presence of my mother or Lukas or me, or the big rig bearing large mechanical treats out in the parking lot, it is not evident.

"Helen," he says in a big soft way like he has not laid eyes on her in ten years. He smiles as broadly as possible, his one-and-a-half stroke smile that is now a thing of stark, chilling worry to see. He was always something of an oddity, but a fun oddity, eccentric when he was part of society, part of the game. Now, though, there are more tics and weaknesses and strangenesses, and the qualities that are not new hang on him differently in this light. He is more like a homeless guy you might want to avoid, a free-walking citizen, but just barely.

"Ah, Gus," Grammus says, equally warmly, but also gesturing up at the wall behind her, up at big her. She is shaking her head like, *why*?

Grampus walks right up close to Grammus, sticks his hand deep into the pocket of his baggy pants, and pulls out a small velvet box.

"Congratulations on winning Employee of the Month for August," he says solemnly, "for making the last month of the summer season the best month of all."

He is holding the little felt box up to her in the shaky white palm of his wide open hand.

Now, my grammus has the ability, like no one else I have met, to be the driver, the cool, comfortable controller of any situation. It is just her way in life, to take it head-on and take it with a laugh, and by doing that, to stay on top of all things. You could knock yourself out cold trying to fluster my grammus.

She is flustered. Her eyes are darting in a guilty and scared search for the right stuff, but the right stuff is hiding from her for once.

"Lukas brought back your things, Gus," she says brightly, shakily.

His hand is still floating there in the air between them. I can see him, though, weakening, his hand sinking as he waits for her to take up her prize.

"Open it," he says, inching the little box farther in her direction.

She shakes her head no, and I can hear the snuffling as Peach begins to cry. The bell on the door rings, and Leonard walks in towing Egon. They freeze just inside.

"Lukas brought your things back, Gus," Grammus says again, getting watery herself now.

Grampus is losing the fight with himself, with gravity and fading strength, as the hand with the box sinks like the big ball on New Year's Eve. With great slow effort he puts the box back in his pocket.

"I don't want any things," he says. "I want you."

"Take the things," Egon blurts, and Leonard bundles him out the door like a bouncer.

Grammus reaches down and takes his hand and squeezes his grip around the box that contains the ring that she is never going to look at. "Summer is over, Gus, and as lovely as the summer was, we all need to get back now to the rest of our lives."

Leonard slips back in, in time to add to the long fat quiet peppered with sniffles. Leonard cries whenever Peach cries, but he doesn't need any encouragement here.

Grampus holds a long pause, then pulls his hand away from Grammus.

"I don't want the rest of my life," he says. "I want the one I had. I want the one I traded away."

That tears it. Nobody can hold it together at this point, and while I'm not saying I'm crying, I'm not saying I'm not crying. Leonard takes a step toward his dad but is stopped with a straight-arm. Instead, Grampus walks around Grammus to his old friend Lukas.

"Big Game of Everything, huh, Luke? Luckie Lukie? You got every last point in the end, didn't you."

"That's not it at all . . . ," Lukas says.

"No, Gus," Grammus says. "All we've tried to do is—"

"Whatever you are trying to do, just stop trying to do it now. I am a stupid old man, but I am just smart enough to know that the things I bought never actually made me happy. The only thing I could do this late in the game to make things any worse would be to take those wicked machines back from you."

They are interrupted by the sound of the digger starting up outside.

"Jock," Grampus snaps, "go tell that mad brother of yours to leave that thing right where it is."

I head for the door, but instantly the bumping, gurgling diesel sound gets louder, grindier, it becomes more frantic, and I do too. I rush out the door to find Egon has lowered the ramp on the truck, and the digger is plowing forward as fast as a digger can. I see him trying to control it, working controls wildly, but the machine has its own plan and not even Egon can alter it.

I chase after the thing pointlessly as it crosses the lot and, like a fullback slaughtering a defensive line, it barrels right into Grampus's workshop.

It's an almighty crash scene when I come up to it, with a crowd following right behind me. The whole forward wall of the shop has been taken out; desk, tools, machinery, everything useful inside crushed under the mighty little contraption. The roof has fallen in. You can see pieces of models and diagrams from Grampus's nutty reinvention of the game of baseball splattered everywhere.

Egon, of course, is fine, because the Egons of the world are always unscratched on the outside, and because the cab cage of the digger is built to withstand having a house dropped on it. Which is pretty much what happened.

Grampus's house. The scene of his inventions. The place of his last great success, and of his next great success. Gone in one quick breath.

Before the shock can even lift from anybody else, Grampus starts laughing. It grows really hard, intense and wheezy, and he laughs and he laughs and he laughs, and you know what? He laughs some more.

I allow myself to wonder briefly if this, finally, is the moment that certifies Grampus as nuts and changes Egon. If the boy can possibly see the damage—physical and otherwise—he has delivered, and feel guilty about it.

"I think I killed the mouse," he says, smiling.

"If nobody else wants the digger, can I have it?"

Nowhere. We have gotten precisely nowhere with him, and why should I have bothered thinking otherwise.

Egon goes on operating the digger, back, forth, sideways, serpentine. Grinding up everything in his path.

I feel my grandfather's weakened, shaky hand grab hold of mine as we stand there watching the horror movie that is Egon.

"Still love my life so much, Jock?" Grampus says.

Is it a joke? Is it a test? I can't figure, but I don't care.

"Yes," I say, "I do."

"I'm one of life's losers, you know. I've always lost at everything, truth be told. Most of my money, my *stuff*, my wife—twice—even starting to lose my hair . . ."

The man does not want my pity. That's the last thing he wants, and he especially doesn't want it when he appears to be asking for it. That's why the crowd starts dispersing at this point, fading back in the direction of the office, because no one wants to entertain this.

Except, uh-uh. Enough. You cannot just stand back while the Teddys and Egons of the world have everything their own way, while the big crowd of everybody else just disperses. At some point you have to push back, or else look forward to a whole lifetime of watching the Teddys and Egons of this world having everything their own way.

"Jeez, Grampus," I say, yanking my hand away from him, "now that you put it that way, I see what you mean. I guess you *are* a loser . . . Did you get any on my hand? Is it contagious?" I'm shaking my hand now, as if to make his loser cooties drop off.

It's a fair guess he did not see that coming.

"Who do you think you are talking to?" he says, already oblivious to the way he just talked to himself.

Egon has stopped working the digger and is sitting rapt, idling, watching.

"Come with me," I say, and I grab my grandfather by the front of his shirt. I tow him out of the remains of his workshop and into the shower of fine summer sunlight. "You see that?" I say, pointing up at the sun.

"Of course I see it," he says, "I'm not demented."

"We'll get to that," I say. "For now, take off that shirt."

He raises an authoritative hand, points at me, and protests. "You just listen to me, young—"

"Right, then," I say, and start yanking the tail of his shirt right up out of his pants. He is weakened, and shocked, so as I work my way up, unbuttoning his buttons, I get very little resistance.

Egon comes running up. "Fight, fight, fight, fight," he chants, circling us like we are in the schoolyard.

"Go get the sun lotion," I say.

He stops. "I'm not slathering," he says.

"Fine. Just get it."

Egon runs over to the shop, throws open the door, and hollers to the assembly inside, "Jock's gone nuts and he's beating up Grampus."

Egon comes running back with a posse like in an Old West movie. By the time he has gotten back, it looks a little worse. I have muscled my grandfather down into the one remaining golf cart he still claims as his, and I am forcing his shoes off of him. His shirt is on the ground behind us. "You . . . like . . . cool . . . feet," I insist as he struggles, squirms, and finally kicks me square in the forehead.

"Go, Grampus," Egon shouts as I stumble back. But I have the shoes in my hands, and I turn to the group.

"You," I say, brandishing a shoe at Lukas. "Thank you for the gesture, but could you please take your toys now and just go?"

Grammus comes up to me, in-charge like.

But she's not. I give her a big hug, squeezing the breath and nonsense out of her before she can speak. "Thank you for coming, Grammus," I say. "You were a lot of fun, have a nice trip back to Florida."

She goes all wide-eyed at me, a mock-mortified expression that looks like it could tip over into the real thing if I push my luck any further.

"That sounded very here's-your-hat-what's-your-hurry," she says.

"Egon could be your hat," I say.

"Nope," she says, kissing my cheek. "I was really just leaving, anyway." As she backs away she pushes a thick wad of cash into my hand. "I can trust you to do something good with this, yes?"

I'm staring at the money, dazzled. "Yes?" I repeat, and shove the dough in my pocket.

Grammus goes to Egon, then to Grampus for a private good-bye. I go to my parents. I am on a roll, and rolling with it. "You, barber," I say, pointing at Leonard, "you have any scissors in there? Go get 'em."

"Yes, sir," says Leonard, always happy to play.

"You, lady," I say to Peach. "We need meat in this place, and we need it now."

Peach leans close and squeezes me, lifting me right off the ground and applying intense, intermittent pressure that makes my limbs shoot out, go limp, shoot out again. "Ain't gonna happen, sweetheart," she says, putting me down. "But otherwise, you are doing very well."

Leonard gives me the scissors. I march toward my grandfather, sitting humbly in his little cart, as the flatbed pulls away with his old toys and the car follows carrying his old flame. I reach him, climb into the seat next to him, and look into his eyes.

"You have not just *started* losing your hair," I say to him, gently but firmly.

His eyes roll upward, toward the white plastic travesty that is his comb-over.

He nods bravely, then closes his eyes tight.

I reach over and, like I'm lifting a manhole cover, pry the solid, shellacky mass from one side of his head until the whole thing is standing upright along the other side. Then, with more difficulty than I would have expected, I force myself to address it, moving closer, closer with the scissors, opening them wide, opening, closing . . .

It must take me a solid three minutes. It's like shearing through a whole side of beef. Each reinforced fiber puts up a mighty battle, each making a nasty crunch sound as I get through.

But then it is done.

Leonard, Peach, and now Meredith are standing applauding the scene, as Grampus gingerly touches the newness of his all-skin head. Egon comes galloping by and snatches the still-complete helmet of hair from me, dumping the sun cream in my lap. He puts the hair on his head for a second, then sails it like a Frisbee.

I reach over and begin applying a healthy layer of UV protection on my grandfather's shiny dome.

"Looks good, Dad," Leonard says, leaning in. "But, I think maybe that fringe could use a little professional touch-up."

Grampus looks to me. "What do you think?"

I squint. It is pretty rough-looking. "Maybe a little."

"We'll meet you at the barbershop," Grampus says, and starts up the cart.

He sets off tooling across the lot, toward the road.

"You're driving all the way there in a golf cart?" I ask.

"Sure," he says, "why not? It's a beautiful day, take

it slow, appreciate the scenery. Squeeze last bits from summer, huh?"

"Sure," I say, shrug, lean back in my seat.

"By the way, Jock, that was some good bossing back there."

"Thanks, Grampus."

"No," he says, "thank you. I feel better. Things feel better. Shirt and shoes off, that was the ticket. That was it, I was too constricted. You'll make a good boss. You'll make a good . . . whatever."

This makes me smile. Whatever it means.

"Hey!" Egon shouts right in Grampus's ear. He is on his bike now, pedaling alongside the cart. "You know that ring you were going to give Grammus. You don't need it, right, so maybe I'll just hold on to it . . ."

Grampus keeps driving, and lays a long, tired look over in my direction.

Right. My brother may in fact wind up being the universe champion at the Big Game of Everything, but it cannot be because I didn't try to save him.

He's my bronion.

"I'll see you later, Grampus," I say. "I have work to do here."

He slaps me on the leg. "Give him one for me."

I bail out my side while the cart is still moving. Egon stops cycling and lays the bike down.

"Hey," he says, balling up a pair of meaty fists as I approach. "You're not the ring, you're the dingleberry."

"Lucky you," I say.

"D'ya love me?" he says, grinning, bouncing, waiting.

"You're not as bad as you seem," I say, proceeding without caution. We are toe-to-toe when he says, "Hey."

I turn to see the sad lumpy figure of Herb Noblett skulking through the heat waves, down the long approach road toward us. We stand watching him, without transport, without his brother, making the endless trip to us.

And without his golf clubs, of course.

"My mom says I have to get my clubs back that you took off me," he says. There is dirt-laced sweat running all down his puggy mug. But there is none of the old menace. Herb the hater of rich kids—whether they are rich or not—is not happy here, but he is not a threat, either.

"They are inside, leaning against the front desk," I say, and he is off to get them.

"He's *whipped*," Egon says, uncommonly impressed. "You know what we should do now, now that he's down? Kick him."

I listen to Egon, but I watch Herb Noblett. Slouched and sweaty, slow and sad. He is whipped.

I pull out the pile of cash Grammus laid on me, and flash it at Egon. He immediately starts panting.

"Where'd you—?"

"I've been saving it. Want to sell me your bike?"

"You already have a bike."

"But yours is nicer."

"Well, duh. That's 'cause *I'm* nicer."

"You know, brother," I say, "if you keep talking, you'll eventually say *everything*."

"Make me."

"Right," I say, recognizing the end of a conversational line when I see one. I peel off far more money than the bike is worth. Egon grabs it and starts his obscene money victory dance.

Noblett comes trudging out of the clubhouse, passing us silently with his bag of clubs and his visible cloud of sweat vapor.

"Here," I say, pushing the bike on him. "This is the replacement for your bike, which my brother lost in the lake."

Egon makes a sound behind me, mid-dance, that is like he somehow got both fists caught in his throat simultaneously.

Noblett stares at me, looking for the joke. When it does not come, he swings a leg over a pretty nice bike, looks all around once more just in case, then glides silently off.

I feel, very plainly, the heat coming off my brother's big red devil head as the two of us stare off at Herb Noblett riding into the not-quite sunset.

"That felt really good," I say, and feel my mouth stretched as wide as possible. "Didn't that feel really good, Egon?"

I hear little puffs of fury at my ear, but no real sound. He's lost his voice from rage.

"D'ya love me?" I ask him.

I can't quite catch his reply, but I know he does.